The Baghdad Mission

The Baghdad Mission

by Sidney and Dorothy Rosen

Carolrhoda Books, Inc./Minneapolis

Adventures in Time Books

Carolrhoda Books, Inc. c/o The Lerner Group
241 First Avenue North, Minneapolis, MN 55401

LIBRARY OF CONGRESS CATALOGING-IN-PUBLICATION DATA

Rosen, Sidney.
  The Baghdad Mission / by Sidney and Dorothy Rosen.
    p. cm.
  Summary: In the year 800, fifteen-year-old Alan travels from the
Frankish kingdom to Baghdad and back again, seeking to escape the
murderous intentions of his evil cousin and secure his birthright.
    ISBN 0-87614-828-3
    [1. Middle Ages—Fiction. 2. Baghdad (Iraq)—Fiction 3. Adventure
and adventurers—Fiction.] I. Rosen, Dorothy. II. Title.
IN PROCESS
[Fic]—dc20   93-36965
                                                            CIP
                                                             AC

Manufactured in the United States of America

1 2 3 4 5 6 - I/BP - 98 97 96 95 94

To our son, David,
a great traveler himself

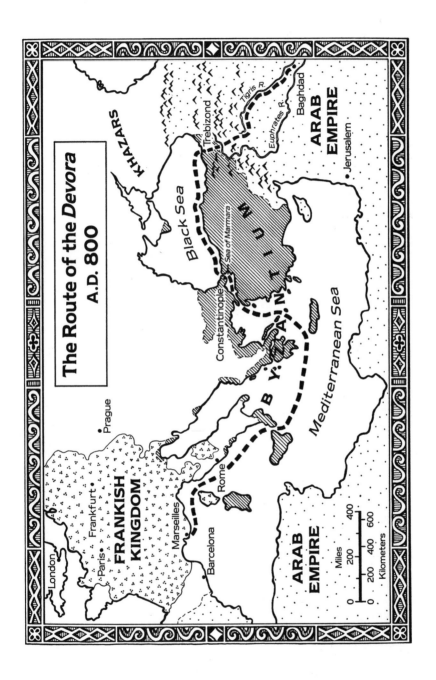

The Route of the Devora
A.D. 800

KHAZARS

Black Sea

Trebizond

Tigris R.

Euphrates R.

Baghdad

ARAB EMPIRE

Jerusalem

Sea of Marmara

Constantinople

B Y Z A N T I U M

Mediterranean Sea

Prague

FRANKISH KINGDOM

London

Paris

Frankfurt

Rome

Marseilles

Barcelona

ARAB EMPIRE

Miles
0   200   400
0   200   400   600
Kilometers

PREFACE

The year A.D. 800 marked the beginning of a time of great change in the history of our world. At that time, the Islamic empire stretched from the sands of Arabia down through present-day Egypt, across North Africa, and up into Spain. The leaders of the empire were called *caliphs* (KAY-liffs). The Abbasid Caliphate made Baghdad, in the area that had once been Persia, the capital of the Islamic empire.

At the height of their domination, the followers of Islam swept across North Africa into Spain, but their advance was halted at the Pyrenees by the leaders of the new Frankish kingdom. The greatest of these, Charles the Great, known in history as Charlemagne (SHAR-leh-main), welded the Franks together politically. Under his leadership, the four hundred years of chaos in Europe that followed the fall of ancient Rome were brought to an end. Now the Christian Church, once only one of many small religious sects, found itself in charge of a new political structure—the western Holy Roman Empire, with Charlemagne as its first emperor. The eastern Holy Roman Empire, in what is now the country of Turkey, was created by Emperor Constantine in A.D. 325. Charlemagne's part of the empire eventually stretched from present-day Italy across Switzerland to Austria and Germany.

Charlemagne's people, the Franks, were a Germanic tribe that had come down into the part of Europe we now call France. The Romans thought of them as barbarians,

but when the Roman Empire collapsed near the end of the fourth century A.D., the Franks took over the territory between Spain and Germany and established their own kingdom.

At the same time, Jewish sailors called Radanites were following trade routes from Europe to Baghdad, India, and China. Historical records show that one Frankish Radanite sailor, called Isaac the Jew, was sent by Charlemagne to Baghdad to serve as an emissary to the Caliph Harun-al-Rashid, the leader of the Islamic empire.

Our story begins in the bleak winter months of this remarkable year in history.

◇ CHAPTER ONE ◇

ast night I swore it on my father's grave on the hill. That someday I'll wring the truth out of Hugo about what really happened there in the deep of the forest. And make him sorry he was ever born!

Alan clenched his fists. He was lying stretched out on the parapet of the castle, tracing out the pattern of Draco the Dragon in the February night sky. Shivering, he pulled his robe closer about him. Already a month since they'd carried his father's body up that hill. The day after Alan's fifteenth birthday in the year 800. His cousin Hugo, six years older than Alan, swore that the whole thing was an accident. Alan's father and Hugo were out hunting in the far western section of the forest. In the

midst of galloping after a boar, the horse stumbled and threw Alan's father into a ravine.

Threw his father? If only he could believe Hugo's story! But there was no better rider in the Frankish Empire than Gerard of Toulon. How could a man who'd ridden to battle with Charlemagne against the Moors be killed like a novice knight? No, there was something that his cousin wasn't telling. Hugo had played a part in his father's death, Alan just knew it.

But there's no proof, he thought bitterly. Oh, why hadn't he seen it coming! The greedy villain wanted all along to get his hands on the estate. And Mother and Father were so trusting, from the day they took Hugo in. He remembered his mother telling him that now he'd have a big brother. That puffed-up braggart his brother? Ha!

Alan pounded a fist against the stone. Nothing had been the same since his father was killed—how could it be? Hugo lorded it over everybody. Insulting Alan openly, calling him a weakling, because he always bested Alan at long sword practice. And Mother did little but stay in her rooms and grieve.

Worst of all was this guilty feeling that stuck to him like a burr. Day and night, whatever he did. Why had he overslept that morning so that they went off to hunt without him? That's what he kept asking himself over and over. Just because his dog Brunhilde took sick and kept him up half the night. Someone must've given her some poisoned food. Could it have been Hugo? Not till sunrise

did she give her tail a wag and Alan's fingers a grateful lick. So he went back to sleep till the uproar in the courtyard woke him. When he looked out the window, there it was, right beneath him. His father's body draped over the horse's saddle.

Now Alan's eyes traced the line from the pointer stars of the Big Bear to the North Star. His father should have been there right beside him the way he used to be, teaching him to recognize the constellations. But even with so many of Gerard's possessions in the castle to remember him by, Alan's father was becoming only a shadow in his mind. Alan could picture the silver wine cup with the handle shaped like a deer and the Moorish scimitar on his bedroom wall. Gerard had captured the scimitar during Charlemagne's campaign in the Pyrenees. A present from his father Alan didn't even know how to use.

And who could Alan speak openly to now? Lothair, the servant who had been with them ever since Alan could remember, was getting old. What could Lothair do about Hugo, anyhow? And Mother? Hugo seemed to be able to get around her whenever he wanted. Now he had wheedled her into agreeing to some kind of risky business, together with the bishop of Toulon. Smooth speeches flowed from the churchman like water down a stream. The two of them had coaxed her into financing a mission to the East, to Baghdad, to bring back silks and spices to sell for big profits. Taking a chance that a Radanite ship

called the *Devora* could perform such a miracle! What did his mother, lost in her grief, know about business?

The moon was just coming up, a crescent shape like his scimitar. One of the dogs in the courtyard was barking, and from the forest Alan could hear the faint hoo-hoo of an owl. Being at the top of the castle seemed to take away some of the ache inside him. Surely his father was in heaven. So maybe Alan was a little closer to him under the winking brightness overhead. He was just beginning to mark out the long star trail of the constellation Hydra, near the southern horizon, when he was startled by a noisy clatter. He heard the scuffling of boots on the stairs, and voices. The footsteps stopped not far away. Alan stayed as motionless as possible.

"Don't worry, we can talk freely. No one comes up here anymore." It was Hugo's nasal voice. "Didn't I tell you the countess would go along with my idea?"

"Good thinking. Now we don't have to risk one silver coin of our own!" The chuckle came from the bishop of Toulon.

"First things first. We've got to get rid of that skinny brat. Alan has to be put out of the way. Then we'll have clear sailing."

The bishop cleared his throat. "But is that so simple? Wouldn't doing away with him lead to—uh—complications?"

They were standing against the battlements. Turning his head a fraction, Alan could see the outlines of their

figures: Hugo's craggy face above solid shoulders and the bishop's belly curving his robe outward. Had he heard right? Alan wondered. His cousin was planning to kill him? Goose bumps popped out on his flesh. Hugo was going to kill him! He lay as motionless as a log, his mind whirling.

Hugo laughed. "Complications? He'll be no trouble at all! That I can guarantee! Many's the time he's tried to best me with the long sword." He guffawed and slapped his thigh. "His every move, weak as a kitten."

"I see." The bishop had a dry voice that became silky whenever he talked to Alan's mother. "But, mind you, the countess must not hear a whit of this. She dotes on Alan like a mother hen."

"Don't worry, I'll manage her." Hugo's voice took on a harsh tone. "Maybe she'll learn to look on me truly as her sister's child. Ever since my parents were killed during the attack on our castle, the whole lot of them has treated me as a charity case. Wait'll she sees me leading an army against Charlemagne himself!" He chuckled half to himself. "Until then, I'll appear to be the faithful nephew comforting her in her grief. She'll be grateful to me even as she's handing over control of the castle. The joke is, having her here puts the stamp of approval on my claim to the castle."

"And has it all been settled with the Radanite captain? The Jew suspects nothing?" asked the bishop.

Hugo snorted. "Suspect me? Of what? No, all he

thinks about is the money the countess has guaranteed for the Baghdad mission. Everyone says the Radanites are the best sailors in the Mediterranean. The risk is small."

"And when they return with the cargo—"

Alan heard the slap of Hugo's hand on the parapet. "We'll have them in our hands!"

Now the bishop chortled. "Well, when I denounce Isaac the Jew as one who sells Christian children into slavery, who's going to question me?"

Hugo joined him in laughter. "Who'd argue with a bishop?"

"No one in Toulon, anyway!" The bishop choked on his own laughter and coughed. "And Simon of Brittany is sure to come in with us?"

"I have his word. He's never forgiven the conquest of his lands by Charlemagne's grandfather. Just as I'll never forget that Charlemagne sent no help when our castle was attacked."

The bishop sighed. "Yes, yes, you've told me the story. Well, then, it's all settled. We'd better return to our chambers before the others awaken."

Alan lay frozen, waiting for their footsteps to subside. When he was satisfied that they were gone, he sprang up. Hugo's ready to kill me, he thought in disbelief. Kill me!

He wanted to scream, to yell, to smash something to pieces, to send a boulder crashing over the battlements onto the heads of those two. He yearned to storm down

the stairs, kick in Hugo's door, and smash his face in. But what if Hugo grabbed his long sword? It would give Hugo just the chance he wanted—to murder Alan and swear it was self-defense, that Alan had attacked him.

He began to pace back and forth, trying to think. The refrain went around and around in his brain: *Hugo's going to kill me.* His hands were icy and his forehead was sweaty. He wiped it with his knuckles. When would Hugo make his move? And how? Would he creep into Alan's room when he was asleep and plunge a knife into his heart? Or would he challenge Alan to long sword practice and turn it into a fight to the death?

Hugo's right, he thought in a panic, *I'm no match for him at all. What can I do?*

He stopped and stared out over the parapet. The sickle moon cast just enough light for him to make out the shapes of trees lining the hill to the family burial plot.

I can't wait too long, he thought. *Now I know Hugo killed my father. That monster! I'll wring the truth out of him someday. Oh, how I'd love to slice that Moorish scimitar through Hugo's neck tonight! Maybe creep into his room after he falls asleep?*

It's only what he deserves. But then, what about the bishop? Kill him, too?

He ran his fingers through his hair. He couldn't do it. He was not a murderer. It was one thing to beat someone in a fair duel. But killing in cold blood? That would make Alan as evil as Hugo. He remembered his father

saying that killing was no pleasure, even though it was a knight's duty in battle.

Just thinking about Hugo sent a wave of heat through him, as if his blood had been stirred and boiled in a cauldron. He took a deep breath. I've got to stay calm or I'll be finished, he told himself. Should he tell his mother about this? But she'd been through so much already. And what could she do to help, anyway? Maybe they could run away from Hugo together. But how could he take her away from her home? They'd be giving up everything Gerard had lived for.

He knew he had to do something—fast. He had to get out of there. That very night. Was he a coward to run and leave his mother behind, with his cousin in control? That hypocrite! That murderer! After everything Alan's parents had done for him! But Mother would be safe. Hugo told the bishop he needed her presence in the castle, to put the stamp of approval on his taking over. Alan was the one he needed to get rid of.

Alan stared out at the hill where his father was buried, next to his little sister, Sophia.

Then he remembered the *Devora* lying at anchor in Marseilles.

◇ CHAPTER TWO ◇

hat's this? A stowaway? Oh, my aching back! Just what we need around here!"

The outcry, followed by a string of oaths, jolted Alan awake. He struggled into a sitting position and rubbed his eyes, blinking at the darkness and the odor of pickles. Where on earth was he?

A foot prodded him. "Get up, you lazy sluggard, get a move on!"

Someone yanked him to his feet and pushed him around. His wrists were clapped together and tied tightly. A hand spun him around again. His captor's broad shoulders were framed against the daylight beyond the doorway, but the face was in shadow. Alan tried to speak

17

but his throat was dry, only a croak came out.

The man bent to snatch up the belt with the scimitar and purse that Alan had removed before falling asleep. Then he shoved Alan out the door into the blinding glare of sunlight and the salty smell of the sea. The sea!

Of course, now it all came back! Last night on the battlements of the castle. Hugo and the bishop of Toulon. *We've got to get rid of that skinny brat.*

Struggling to keep his feelings in check, he had stopped only long enough to whisper to Lothair a message for his mother telling her not to worry, he was going on a secret pilgrimage in his father's name. Then he had stolen out of the castle, silent as a thief, ridden to Marseilles, and crept aboard the *Devora*. Of course, he was taking a big chance. Would the man called Isaac the Jew believe his story? Surely Isaac would be grateful to hear of Hugo's treachery, and he would treat Alan as a royal passenger. The Radanite ship would be his refuge.

Now his captor was pulling him roughly along. The rope was chafing his wrists. They were in a long passageway below the deck, where two lines of rowers sat naked to the waist, silent and listless over their still oars. The stink of their sweat filled Alan's nostrils.

"Here, you, up you go!" He was being hauled up a short flight of stairs to the deck, where he was flung down like a sack of meal. The man planted a sandaled foot on his chest. "Captain!" he yelled. "Come and have a look at what I found! You won't believe it!"

Above Alan a great square of white sail billowed against the blue of the sky. His back ached, and his captor's sandal was squeezing the air out of his lungs. My God, he thought, was I a fool to stow away on this ship? What will they do to me?

At least he could see his captor now. His red beard and hair stood out against his dark tunic and bronzed muscular arms. A sheathed scimitar hung from his belt. The man was staring at Alan with disgust. Other faces formed a circle around Alan, all bearded and fierce looking, except for one beardless face on a boy about his own age. A babble of voices sounded in his ears.

"An extra mouth to feed? Toss him overboard!"

"He's blond like the Saxon slaves. But this one's too skinny to be useful!"

The circle parted and another figure loomed over him, this one taller and slimmer than the first, and older, with a dark beard in which a few white hairs glistened. He wore a belted scimitar, too. He motioned to Alan's captor.

"Saul, let the boy up." The foot came away, and Alan sat up coughing. He wanted to put a hand to his mouth, but the tug told him his wrists were still tied behind his back.

"Well, young man, can you give me one good reason why I shouldn't have you thrown to the fishes?" The older man bent and pulled Alan to his feet. "Speak up!"

"I—you see—it's just—" What could he say? He didn't

know where to begin. His legs felt weak, and the swaying of the deck was making him dizzy.

"Who needs a reason?" Red-beard snorted. "He's a
stowaway, isn't he? Jason's right, Isaac, we don't need
another mouth to feed!"

Isaac. The Radanite captain who was to carry out
Hugo's mission. Was he a murdering liar like Hugo?

Alan's mouth was dry. He licked his lips and tried not
to show how scared he was. What was this sea captain
going to do? Would he let his tough crew toss him overboard? Red-beard poked him in the ribs and pointed
down a hatch toward the rowers. "See those Saxons,
boy?"

Alan nodded, gazing at the fair-haired captives.

"Stowaways have to earn their keep. One way is to join
that gang of slaves!"

In dismay Alan eyed the naked backs bent over the oars,
wet with perspiration. He could see the light glinting off
the iron cuffs of their wrist and ankle chains. Was Red-
beard serious?

In spite of the sunshine, Alan couldn't help shivering.
He had hidden aboard the *Devora* to find a haven. And
now he was worse off than ever, on this ghastly ship where
everyone was an enemy. Would he be chained to a bench,
arms straining and pulling at an oar?

Would he end up a slave?

And all this was happening on account of that murdering Hugo! One more blow to be repaid!

CHAPTER THREE

The captain reached over and pinched Alan's arm. "A rower? Come, Saul, muscles like this couldn't lift an oar one inch!" He turned to the other sailors. "All right, back to work, everyone. I'll handle this."

With one hand on Alan's shoulder, the captain steered him toward a cabin near the ship's bow. Inside, he motioned him to a built-in wooden bench. He stood towering over him, frowning.

The captain's silence was more alarming than Redbeard's oaths. What was in the mind of this tall man with the dark, piercing eyes? Would he believe Alan's story?

"I don't know why you picked my ship, lad," began the captain, pacing back and forth, "but you've brought

us a pack of trouble. If we go about to bring you back to Marseilles, we lose time. And time is money. If you stay, you'll have to work your passage, skinny or not. You're an extra mouth to feed. So we'll have to take on more provisions at our next port of call. More money wasted.

"Worst of all, sailors are superstitious. My men are already convinced that a stowaway jinxes the entire voyage. Boy, you're a problem I don't need!"

Alan felt his face grow hot. "I—I'm sorry. It seemed like the only way out."

"Only way out? Out of what? And why the *Devora*? Speak up, boy! What's your name?"

I'm a nobleman's son, Alan thought. This captain is only a commoner. And not even a Christian. He'd better not make me a slave!

He jumped to his feet and drew himself up as tall as he could. "I'm Alan, count of Toulon! If you don't release me at once, you'll have to answer to Charlemagne himself!" It wasn't easy to act like a nobleman with his hands tied behind his back.

Was that the glimmer of a smile on the captain's rather wide mouth? "Oh? And your father is...?"

"Was. Gerard of Toulon. And my cousin is Hugo, someone you know only too well."

The captain's dark eyes took on a hooded look. Slowly he pulled his scimitar from its sheath.

Alan's heart sank. He's going to do what the crew

wants. Get rid of me. But I'm not going to beg for my life! And where can I run on a ship?

"Turn around, boy."

He closed his eyes and turned, silently saying a prayer.

Suddenly his hands came free. The scimitar had cut the rope. Alan gulped with relief and turned. The captain motioned with his hand. "Sit down, lad." He sat opposite Alan. "Hugo came by this morning with some armed men looking for you. Luckily, no one knew you'd come aboard. We were all in town trading for new rowers. Tell me, why is he hunting you? What are you running away from?"

"My cousin Hugo was getting ready to kill me, that's what!" Alan sucked in his breath. "He and the bishop of Toulon were talking about it as if Hugo were going to hunt partridges! Hugo's always been jealous of me, ever since my parents took him in. And now that my father's dead, he wants to murder me and take over my father's castle and land. Make himself the new count of Toulon!"

Captain Isaac's eyebrows rose. "Well, well. How do you know all this?"

The words tumbled out. "Last night I was up on the castle battlements watching the stars...." He told the captain what he had overheard.

"He's going to fight Charlemagne? Our King Charles? Are you sure?"

"That's what they said! Hugo's always hated Charlemagne. For not helping his family when their castle was

attacked years ago. Truth is, the king was away fighting the Saxons then.''

The captain shook his head. "He's an ambitious one, that Hugo. Trying to pull down Charlemagne himself.''

"And that's not all." Alan stopped to take a deep breath. "After you come back from this mission, they're going to cheat you out of everything! They'll sell the goods and use the money to raise their army!''

The captain's eyes narrowed. "Cheat me? Did they say how?''

"The bishop is going to swear that you sell Christian children as slaves! The bishop and Hugo will keep all the profits and you'll end up...." The words trailed off. Alan bit his lip.

"Hanging at the end of a rope, is that what you mean?'' Isaac's eyes narrowed.

Alan nodded.

"While Hugo and the bishop, good Christians both, prosper.'' The captain was leaning forward intently, one hand plucking at his beard. "That part about enslaving Christian children, boy. You're certain about that?''

Alan nodded again.

"Well, Alan of Toulon, that's quite a story. But how do I know that you're telling the truth? Your Hugo's a crafty scoundrel. Maybe he put you up to this, to keep an eye on me?''

Alan stared at him. "On my father's honor, it's all true, every word. Why would I run away and leave my mother

alone in Hugo's hands? I love my mother, Captain Isaac. She's all I have now. I only pray she'll be safe."

The captain drummed his fingers on the table. "Well, lad, knowing your cousin, it all seems to fit together. Don't know why I agreed to go on this mission in the first place. I just couldn't resist a chance to get back to Baghdad. And what that bishop of yours is planning has an all-too-familiar ring. Still, I'm not certain...."

Alan jumped to his feet. "Honest, Captain, I swear by the Holy Virgin...."

The captain held up a hand. "You say they're planning to raise an army against Charlemagne?"

Alan nodded vigorously. "That's right. They hate Charlemagne! So does Simon of Brittany. He's going to join them as soon as they get their army together. They all bear grudges against the king. They're either furious with him or jealous."

The captain's long fingers plucked at his beard again. "Old stories, I hear them over and over. More than one knight has dreamed of carving out a piece of the kingdom for himself. Well, all of that will have to wait. It'll be quite a while before we get back to Marseilles."

"How long, sir?"

"Mm, at least a year."

"A year!"

"Why do you look so surprised, lad? We're on our way to Baghdad. That's not just around the next headland, you know." Isaac marked the places off on his fingers.

"First, Constantinople in Thrace. Then, across to Trebizond. Then we leave the ship and go by caravan across the mountains. Then through the desert along the Tigris River to Baghdad. My lad, we're talking about hundreds of leagues there and hundreds back! And, we Radanites travel faster than most merchants."

A whole year! Alan sat there stunned by this news. Why hadn't he stopped to figure things out? He thought of his last moonlit glimpse of the castle turrets, with Lothair keeping the whining Brunhilde from dashing after him. He only stopped once, at the graves of his father and his little sister, where he'd said a farewell prayer before galloping on to Marseilles. "It worries me terribly, leaving my mother behind with Hugo in charge," he said slowly.

"Don't worry, lad. It strikes me that Hugo will treat your mother well. And he'll have good reason. Having her alive and well in the castle puts the stamp of legitimacy on his claim. So put your mind at rest on that score."

"I hope you're right." A whole year on this journey! Would he ever get back to settle the score with Hugo?

The captain's deep voice broke into his thoughts. "Are you hungry, Alan of Toulon?"

"Starving. I've had nothing to eat or drink since supper last night."

"Come—" The captain stood and led him back across the deck to the larger cabin. The Radanite sailors glanced at them with curious eyes. Inside the cabin, a wizened

cook called Moises was told to feed him.

Before he left, the captain asked, "Alan, have you ever been on a ship like this?"

"No, sir."

"Well, you'll have plenty of time to get to know the *Devora*." Isaac started to leave, then turned and shook his finger at him. "Remember, lad, nobleman or commoner, everyone here earns his keep. Saul's the bos'n, you'll take your orders from him." A frown wrinkled his brow. "And you'd better obey him to the letter!"

In the stuffy little galley, Moises gave Alan a toothless grin and set down before him a bowl of thick porridge, chunks of dark bread, and an apple. "Don't worry about the cap'n, boy. He's a good man, he'll treat you fair and square. But watch out for that bos'n!"

Alan didn't have to be told. While shoveling the food down as fast as he could, he was already dreading what had to come next—facing Red-beard. What would the bos'n expect from him? Alan had never even set foot on a ship before.

A head with curly red hair escaping from a close-fitting blue cap appeared in the doorway. "Hey, stowaway, you finished yet?" The voice belonged to the boy he had noticed on deck before. Alan nodded. "C'mon, Saul wants you right away."

Outside, Alan followed the boy, who was dressed in a blue tunic tied with a rope belt. *He's a lot smaller than I am,* he thought. *Puny, too, for heavy work on a ship*

this big.

"What's your name?" Alan asked. "What do you do around here?"

"I'm Ray. Cabin boy. What's yours?"

"Alan. How old are you?"

"None of your business! I'm old enough."

"Just asking. I'm fifteen. What are you so angry about?"

"You're a stowaway. Stowaways bring bad luck!"

"How do you know that?"

"Jason said so. Everyone else, too. Said you'd take the food out of our mouths. Said you ought to be heaved overboard!"

Alan bit his lip. Wasn't he going to find even one friend on this ship? And Ray seemed to be the only one near his age. "Don't worry. I'll earn my passage. And I'll pay for the extra food at our next stop." He held out his hand. "Friends?"

Ray slapped it away. "No stowaway's *my* friend!"

The rejection stung Alan. Well, he could get along without this nasty-tempered fellow. "If that's the way you feel...." He shrugged.

They had reached the spot where Saul was standing with his back toward them. He was gazing up at the great sail that was curved out by the wind.

"Here's the stowaway."

Saul turned and smiled at Ray. Then he did something that left Alan standing there with his mouth open. He

laid one hand on the boy's head and stroked it gently. "Thank you, daughter."

Daughter? This was Saul's daughter? "So Ray isn't short for Raymond?"

"No, ninny, it's Rae for Rachel."

This "cabin boy" was a girl!

◇ CHAPTER FOUR ◇

Moises, the little cook with leathery skin as wrinkled as a baked apple, proved to be Alan's first friend aboard ship. "Try this, it'll put hair on your chest," he would coax, setting down a bowl of steaming soup. "You'll be able to keep this down, wait and see." The same encouraging words always followed his chuckle. "You'll get your sea legs one of these days, mark my words!"

Alan would groan and pick up the bowl. Maybe he could manage the broth, after all.

In addition to all his other problems, he'd had to deal with seasickness. Every time his face turned green and he dashed for the ship's side, all the other sailors split their

sides laughing. But after losing too many meals this way, Alan decided to watch the other sailors and see how they managed. They certainly enjoyed their meals and kept the food down. He wanted desperately to do the same.

As Alan slowly sipped Moises's broth, he began to remember what it was like to ride his mare, Star. Riding meant bobbing up and down. Bobbing while riding had never bothered him. And that was the way the ship was moved by the waves. So why not imagine that instead of being at sea, he was riding horseback? In his mind, the sails and mast could become an archway of tangled branches and green leaves swaying above him.

"Moises, your soup just gave me a brilliant idea!" He dashed out.

And it worked! He was never sure why. Did the seasickness stop because of his imaginary riding? Or had he simply gotten used to the ship's motion? Perhaps being ashamed of being different did the trick. But who cared what the reason was? Now he could finish a meal and go darting about the deck like the others, even in foul weather. He felt proud of this first victory.

But there were chores to do that strained every muscle. At the castle, all he'd ever had to do was rub down Star after riding. Plenty of servants were around to take care of every task. Now he was amazed at all the work that had to be done by the crew each day aboard ship: the long wide deck to be scrubbed clean every day, ropes to be spliced and coiled, crew and rowers to be fed, sacks and

casks of food to be hauled up from the hold, the mast to be climbed, the sail to be reefed and lowered, knots to be tied, the heavy steering oar to be kept in place, and fish to be caught for dinner. Most of the tasks were completely foreign to Alan.

No wonder Jason and the others had bulging muscles. Jason was one of the noisy young sailors who had called for tossing Alan overboard. He was tall and lean, with a scar cutting across one tanned cheek. Alan still cringed inwardly when he remembered how the captain had pinched his arm and remarked on its flabbiness. It's true, he thought, my muscles are pathetic compared to the others. How will I ever get the best of Hugo?

Alan's lack of muscle showed up in embarrassing ways. He failed at practically everything he tried. Tasks that sounded easy proved just the opposite. One morning when Saul ordered him to go aft and help Jason with the steering oar, Alan ran eagerly to the stern. Just keeping that big oar in place didn't sound like much of a challenge.

Jason didn't seem eager to have Alan's help. No smile lit his face. "Saul sent you? Well, grab hold."

When Alan obeyed, he found that the steering oar was much longer and fatter than he had thought. It rested in the deep groove of a large wooden block nailed to the side of the stern. "Look sharp," Jason warned. "We've got to keep 'er headed into the waves. If we let 'er go broadside, they'll swamp us!"

Alan clamped his fingers around the oar and pushed

or pulled whenever Jason did. The job's really not so tough, he thought. But a little later, Jason said, "Hold 'er for a minute, will you? Got to go below. Be right back."

"Sure, Jason." Alan was positive he could handle the steering. It was easy. Just a little push or a pull would keep the ship on a steady path.

But even as the thought crossed his mind, the sea shoved the oar to one side, almost wresting it from his grasp. He tried to push the other way, but he couldn't budge it. The oar seemed to be glued in the wrong direction. Straining with all his might, he leaned into the oar, struggling to push it against the grip of the water. It was no use. Little by little, the ship veered away from its true course and started a slow roll in the troughs of the waves. The sail began to flap loudly as it lost wind.

A shout went up from near the bow. "Port side, oars out! Hold them in the water!"

Red-bearded Saul came rushing over to where Alan was fighting the steering oar. "What's the matter, boy, can't you keep that oar straight? Didn't you see the sail luffing?" He pushed Alan out of the way and grabbed the oar, giving it a mighty heave. The ship's roll lessened, the sail caught the wind and popped out. The prow rose and fell once more as the ship headed back into the waves. The bos'n turned his head and roared, "Ship oars!" The order was repeated below middeck, where the rowers sat.

Jason came running back. "What happened?" He grabbed on to the steering oar and helped Saul push.

"What *happened*?" Saul asked. "You left this weakling alone at the oar, that's what! Don't ever do that again! He'll turn us upside down! We'll end up swimming to Constantinople!"

"Saul, I had to go below, just for a second. Thought the kid could handle it." Jason scowled at Alan.

"I'm sorry." Sweating with embarrassment, Alan was ready to leap into the sea and disappear. They were labeling him a weakling, just as Hugo had.

"All right, Jason, take over." Saul turned to Alan. "Let me see your hands, boy!" After he'd inspected them, he said, "Not used to hard work, are they?" He stuck his face close to Alan's. "Come with me!"

The bos'n led Alan down the deck to a pail half-filled with water. Next to it was a big piece of pumice stone and a lump of brown soap. He pushed the pumice toward Alan with his foot. "Here! Swab this part of the deck, all the way to the mast. And when you finish, I want it shiny enough to see your face in!"

Red-faced, Alan sank to his knees and started scrubbing. The hot Mediterranean sun seemed to burn through his thin tunic and scorch him. What an idiot he'd been! On the way to Marseilles, he'd imagined the captain would be so grateful to hear about the plot that he'd treat Alan like royalty. Instead, here he was, being worked harder than a serf on his father's estate.

Worse than the scorn being heaped on him was the guilt eating away inside him. Try as he might, he could not

shut out thoughts of his mother. Her face, pale with the haunted look that had lingered since his father's death, kept floating before Alan's eyes and blotting out the horizon. If he had only taken a few moments to wish her a proper farewell, one that she deserved! Yes, maybe he really was the coward Hugo thought him, to leave her in the night without a word.

What would his father have advised him to do that night on the battlements, Alan asked himself, if he could have spoken to Alan from heaven? Perhaps he knew him too well to have any bright hopes for his son's future. How disappointed he used to look, watching him at swordplay with Hugo! Alan always ended up the loser, pinned against the wall. Was his father already worried that someday he'd let the castle and all his lands slip away? And leave Mother helpless, dependent on Hugo's charity?

It was a bitter thought. Silently he vowed that one day he'd go back to the castle and make things right again. Even if he died doing it.

Now he was surrounded by people who despised him for his weakness. Well, he'd show them, whatever it took. Even if it meant working till his muscles screamed for mercy. He could do whatever that bos'n's daughter could!

But his worst moment was yet to come.

A few days after the steering-oar incident, Saul called Alan over to the mast and pointed upward. As bos'n, Saul assigned the tasks on the *Devora*. He stood solid as a tree trunk, feet planted apart for the roll of the ship. His

mouth curved downward in an expression that was already familiar to Alan. It was Saul's let's-see-how-you-handle-this-one look. Rae and a couple of the sailors busied themselves nearby, coiling some rope while they watched with smirks on their faces.

"Here's something every seaman has to learn. Let's see you climb the mast, boy. Up to the top yardarm!"

Alan squinted up at the thick round pole that loomed in the blue sky. His heart sank. Two lines sloped down from the top of the mast to the deck, where they were tied to hooks. A narrow woven ladder also stretched down the same way. He knew it was strong enough to carry his weight. He'd seen big sailors climb it. But now, as he shielded his eyes from the sun and gazed up at the ladder, the higher it went, the more it seemed to become as thin and fragile as a spider's web.

The top yardarm was the spar supporting the top of the sail. To Alan, that long, thin piece of wood seemed as far away as the ghostly sliver of a moon that was stuck in the daytime sky. He hesitated a moment, took a deep breath, and forced himself to move. First, his right foot on the bottom rung. Then the other foot up onto the next. Much more slowly than a spider, Alan edged his way, rung by rung, toward the top. It seemed to him that he'd been climbing for hours when he stopped. He couldn't be any more tired than if he'd been climbing the Alps. Then he looked down.

To his horror, the deck with everyone on it had shrunk

to a miniature size. Not only that, everything was swaying from side to side. Suddenly he was engulfed by a wave
of dizziness. He was going to fall. In desperation he
closed his eyes, flung his arms about the mast, and crushed
his body against it.

Keep going, you're halfway there, he told himself. But
his body refused to listen. He simply could not go any
higher. After a moment, with his eyes still clamped shut,
he felt with one foot for a lower rung. Slowly, one rung
at a time, he crept back down to the deck. It was not until he got to the bottom of the ladder that he dared to open
his eyes again. What a relief to feel solid planks beneath
his feet again! He heaved a big sigh.

Saul and the other sailors all had big grins on their faces.

Rae giggled and pointed. "Look at him, he's as pale
as a ghost!" She jumped to her feet. "Want to see how
it's done, landlubber?" With one leap, she fastened
herself onto one of the lines leading to the top. Hand over
hand like a monkey, she swung herself quickly all the way
up. Then, even faster, she slid back down again.

Jason stopped coiling rope and pointed a finger at Alan.
"Bet that's something blue-blooded noblemen never learn
to do." Everyone laughed.

Rachel stood facing Alan, hands on hips and feet apart,
a smaller imitation of her father. Her green eyes mocked
him. "I suppose you can't help it—you're a landlubber,
poor thing!"

If he had disliked Rae before, now he hated her.

◇ CHAPTER FIVE ◇

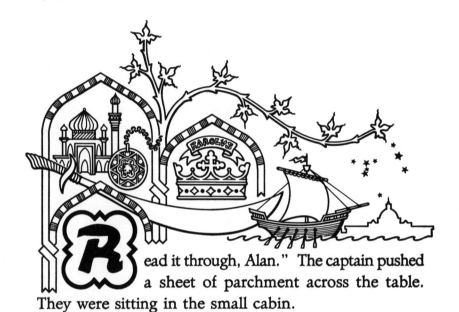

ead it through, Alan." The captain pushed a sheet of parchment across the table. They were sitting in the small cabin.

"What is this, sir?"

"The contract every Radanite has to sign. It's the law. This contract states the terms of your tour of duty. Read it carefully before you sign it. Take your time. If you have any questions, feel free to ask."

Alan's heart sank. Here was more of his ignorance to be shown up! Would the beating his pride was taking aboard the *Devora* never stop?

He had never learned to read.

"Sitting in school is for monks!" his father used to say.

"Noblemen have to spend their time preparing themselves for battle. So they can defend their castles and families!"

Gerard of Toulon himself could barely read and couldn't write at all. But he had always accomplished what he set out to do. He won glory on the battlefield, a glory that also won him the prize of extensive, valuable lands.

Once when Alan asked about learning to read, Gerard had snapped, "What does book learning have to do with being a knight? If I need reading or writing done, I just call Father Paulus from the abbey. And that's what you'll do when you become count of Toulon!"

So Alan had never gone to the cathedral school, where the young monks took lessons in reading, writing, and arithmetic.

Now, facing the captain, he was ashamed to tell him the truth.

He picked up the parchment and looked at it. The sheet was covered with writing in a flowing script. He stared at the sheet with its meaningless squiggles and at the pot of ink and the quill pen on the table. Am I the only one on the *Devora* who can't read or write, he wondered. What shall I do? He glanced at the captain, who sat watching him and stroking his beard. Shall I pretend to read what's written here? And then try to write my name? Father Paulus once taught me how, but I haven't done it in a long time.

"Well? Something wrong, lad?" The captain's voice interrupted his thoughts. "What's the trouble?"

"Nothing! It's just...." Alan kept staring at the parchment. What had possessed him to stow away on this Radanite ship! He picked up the pen. His hand hovered over the parchment.

"What's the matter, Alan?" The dark eyes were examining him.

Slowly he put the pen down. "It's just...." The words wouldn't come. "You see—"

The captain sat back, his thick black eyebrows raised. "Aha! You've never learned to read and write, is that it?"

Alan reddened. "I wanted to go to school. But my father thought learning to fight was what mattered to a nobleman."

"Ah—" The captain pursed his lips. "You mustn't blame him, he was only doing what he thought best for you. It's not easy being a father. I should know, I've made my share of mistakes." His eyes looked opaque and sad.

"You?" Alan was surprised. "But you have to be away from home so much, it must be hard."

"Well, that doesn't help, certainly. For instance, like every father, I was anxious for my firstborn, Reuben, to be a success. He was so quick, so bright!" He was silent for a minute, his fingers drummed on the table. "He wanted to be an artist, a sculptor. Gifted, too. But I showed him there was no future there. He'd always be dependent on the whims of a noble patron. So he listened to me. He became a merchant. And he was a

great success, in no time!"

"So you were right," Alan said, puzzled.

The captain sighed. "Yes, I was right. But he traveled to Naples on business for what was supposed to be a short visit. He caught a fever and died there. He was so young, and all alone, without one member of the family near him. I've blamed myself ever since."

"But it wasn't your fault, that could happen anywhere," Alan said.

"So I tell myself," the captain said dryly. "Well, enough of confessions. You must understand that for a Jew, nothing is more important than learning. Even I, a mere merchant, can read and write Latin, Arabic, and Hebrew. Our King Charles has seen the importance of written language, and even our own Frankish is being written using Latin as a model. On a mission like ours, it's always better if you can talk to a man in his own tongue. It can even be a matter of life and death to understand signs or documents in a foreign land. Tell me again, how old are you?"

"Fifteen."

The captain squinted at him. "Tall for your age. With that blond hair and those blue eyes, you look more like a Saxon than a Frank." He stood up. "Well, lad, it's high time you learned your letters. No one stays illiterate on a Radanite ship! And there's no time like the present." He moved to the door and stuck his head out. "Jason! Find Rachel and tell her I want to see her immediately!"

Then he came back and seated himself.

Alan moistened his lips. Was that haughty girl going to be the one to teach him to read and write? Bad enough that she'd seen him clinging panic-stricken to the mast. Now the captain was going to put her in charge of his education.

She stood in the doorway. "You wanted to see me, Captain?"

"Ah, come in. Rachel, you're going to have a special assignment." He inclined his head toward Alan. "Seems that this fellow hasn't learned to read or write. So you're going to be his teacher. What do you think of that?"

Rae frowned. "Of course, Captain. As you wish." Alan was still seated, and she was looking down at him.

The captain rose. "I'll let you two work out the details. Mind you, I want to see results. So every day, when your regular tasks are done, you two will work on this together. Understood?" His eyes went from Rachel to Alan.

Barely glancing at each other, they both nodded. Rae's lips curved in that superior smile. She loomed over Alan.

He stared back at her. Maybe, he said to himself, it would have been better if they'd tossed me into the sea after all.

◇ CHAPTER SIX ◇

Every evening Alan sat opposite Rae at the rough table in the stuffy cabin, his long legs cramped. Over and over he copied each of the 23 letters of the Roman alphabet on a wax slate. Alan recognized very little Latin. He remembered a few Latin phrases Father Paulus had recited in church, but he had never even tried to read the religious scriptures himself.

First Rae would scratch out a letter on her slate with a sharp stylus and speak the letter's sound, "A." Then Alan drew what he saw.

"No, not like that! Keep the sides straight!"

Did she have to be so fussy? With a groan, he would

use his erasing knife to scrape away his miserable imitation of an *A* and try again. There were so many letters to learn. At this rate, he thought, I'll have a long white beard before we're finished.

His teacher was merciless, forcing him to copy letters over and over until they were perfect. "I suppose a nobleman can't be expected to do a scholar's work." Her sarcasm didn't improve his printing.

Why did she criticize him constantly? Was it to show how much she disliked him? Alan gritted his teeth and sweated over the slate. I'm not going to let her get the better of me, he told himself. And finally, the tiresome beginnings led to some satisfying results. Little by little he caught on. He began to enjoy seeing how the letters could be put together to make words. And how those words could form sentences. One evening as they worked in the musty cabin by the light of the oil lamp, he gazed proudly at his handiwork: *SUPRA DEVORA ALAN NAUTH EST.*

His longest sentence!

"'Alan is a sailor on the *Devora*,'" he translated. "How's that?" With a grin of triumph, he showed his masterpiece to his teacher. To his amazement, she actually smiled at him. Her green eyes gleamed and her red curls caught the light as she pulled off her cap. Surprised, he realized how pretty Rae was, with those tendrils of hair fanned against her smooth cheeks. "Pretty good for a beginner, right?"

Her smile disappeared. "Not bad. But don't fool yourself. Those are only simple words. You still have a long way to go."

He sighed. His strict taskmaster was back, frown and all. But for one moment he had pierced her armor. Suddenly he was seized with a fierce determination. *I'll show her I'm not the spoiled nobleman she thinks I am! Somehow I'll get her to change the way she treats me. Even if I have to outdo every Radanite sailor on the ship. And stay up all night drawing these dumb letters!*

Rae put away the slates. "Well, that's it. We've done enough for tonight."

"Just a second. There's something I'd like to ask you about."

Her eyes opened wide. They'd never spoken to each other about anything except the letters. She'd made it plain that she was in his company strictly because of the captain's orders. "Well?"

"How is it we never have a lesson on Friday nights?"

She pursed her lips. "Do you miss having a lesson, then?" Her eyes mocked him.

"Well, it's not that." Why did she make him feel tongue-tied? "It's that ritual I see the crew and the captain going through after sundown. You know what I mean."

He thought about the Friday night supper when Captain Isaac would set a great silver candelabra with two candles on the table. Rae would cover her head with a

shawl and use a small lighted candle to light the other two. Then she'd mutter a prayer while making fluttery motions with her hands in front of her eyes. The captain would hold up a silver cup filled with wine, chant a prayer, and sip the wine. The silver cup was passed all around. Only then would they begin the special supper—soup and braided bread, baked fish, stewed fruit, and marvelous sticky sweets.

An odd group, these Radanite Jews, thought Alan. Finding God under the open sky, not in a church, without even a priest to lead them.

Now Rae scowled at him. "Stop daydreaming! I just asked, don't you even know about the Five Books of Moses?"

He shook his head. "Never heard of them."

"'Course you have. Only you people give it a different name. The Old Testament in the Bible, you know that! Well, the first part's Genesis, remember? How God made the world."

"I know that much! It took Him six days!"

"And what happened on the seventh?"

He thought a moment. "He rested."

"Right! And that's what we celebrate from sundown Friday to sundown Saturday. It's our Sabbath." A half-smile curved her lips as she talked, her eyes held little points of light.

"But what about Sunday?"

She squinted at Alan. "Yes, the Christian Sabbath. I

once asked Captain Isaac about that. Seems it was the emperor Constantine who changed the day of rest from Saturday to Sunday for Christians. Almost five hundred years ago—"

"Oh? But what's that you do over the candles before Friday night supper?"

"A blessing. To welcome the Sabbath. My mother taught me how to do it."

"Your mother? How come you don't stay home with her?"

She stared at him, her eyes green and cold like the sea. "My mother's dead. And I'm an only child."

A pang went through Alan. "My father just died."

Her mouth opened and closed again. She said nothing. They just sat there. The oil lamp sputtered. The only other sounds were the slap of the oars against the water and the drum beating out the time for the rowers. "Is that why you ran away from home?"

"Maybe—" He hesitated. How much should he tell her? "Well, not that exactly. The truth is, someone was going to kill me if I stayed."

"Kill you? Who? Who was it?"

Why had he brought the whole thing up? How could he explain to this daredevil that he hadn't been up to a duel with Hugo? "It's a whole big mess. One of these days, I'll get back and clean it up. And take care of my mother." He gave a sigh. "A girl without a mother must be as bad as a boy without a father."

Her chin went up. "I know how to take care of myself. I'm no crybaby."

Alan shrugged.

She fiddled with her slate. "Got any brothers or sisters?"

"A little sister, Sophia, but she died." A thought struck him. "She was like you, sort of. Kind of stubborn—had a mind of her own. Always tagging after me. Loved to climb trees but hated embroidery and all that. A tomboy, my mother called her." He stopped, thinking that he was glad he had always let Sophia tag along and play with him and Leon, Lothair's grandson.

"You two!" They both started. Saul was standing in the doorway, his brow furrowed. "What's going on? Isn't the lesson over? It's getting late. Come on, Rachel, time to quit." He stood there frowning at Alan, while Rae gathered up her things and followed him out. She didn't say good-night or even glance back.

What was bothering Red-beard? Rae's father had never come to fetch her before. What was so bad about just talking to Rae for a few minutes after the lesson?

That night it was Alan's turn to stand watch. They had already sailed around Sicily and were now headed directly east. This course, the captain had explained, would bring them to the Aegean Sea. From there they would head

northeast to Constantinople.

The night was pleasantly cool and cloudless. After a while, Alan lay on his back and looked up at the stars blinking above. With the coming of night the wind had died, and the sail was furled. He could hear the rhythmic splash of the oars dipping to the steady beat of the drum.

He spotted the Big Bear to the north, with its two stars that pointed straight to the North Star. Over the western horizon was the constellation Canis Major, the Big Dog. On a frosty night long ago in Toulon, his father had first pointed out Sirius, the brightest star in the Big Dog. The stars are the torches of the angels who watch over us, his father had told him. Was father one of that band of angels now?

But tonight there was something wrong with Sirius. Little by little, it was moving in a northerly direction. The stars were supposed to be fixed in their places in the great starry sphere. So why did Sirius appear to be moving?

Suddenly he realized what was happening. He scrambled to his feet, ran to the fo'c'sle, and shouted for Saul.

The bos'n came out rubbing his eyes. "What's the matter, Alan? What's going on?"

"The stars, look at the stars. Something's wrong!"

"What?" He grabbed Alan by the shoulders and shook him. "Make sense, boy! What about the stars?"

"Sirius—it's moving out of place—look!" Alan pointed upward.

"Sirius?" Saul glanced upward. "Oh, my God!" He dashed toward the stern. Following him, Alan saw a figure draped over the steering oar. The helmsman was snoring, fast asleep. And the steering oar was pushed into a position that was turning the ship to a southerly course.

"Samuel, wake up! We'll end up in Africa!" Saul shouted. He pushed the helmsman off the oar. With Alan's help, he began to turn the ship in the opposite direction. Samuel sat dazed on the deck, rubbing his eyes.

By now, the captain and other crewmen surrounded them. Jason relieved Alan and Saul at the oar. Samuel got to his feet. "Oh, Captain Isaac, I don't know what happened to me, falling asleep like that. I can't believe it!" A flood of apologies poured from him as he wrung his hands.

"There's no excuse for what happened!" The captain's tone was grim. "Who knows how far south we've strayed! And I don't have to remind you what that means. The closer to Africa, the higher the risk of running into Arab pirates!"

Samuel moistened his lips. "In all these years, I've never done anything like this, you know that." He shook his head. "Must've been the drumbeat—it lulled me."

The captain cut him off. "Once is enough, the damage is done. We'll say no more about it. How on earth did you notice it, Saul?"

"The boy, here, woke me up. Seems he was studying the stars and realized we were off course—thank God!"

Saul clapped Alan on the back. The others all stared at Alan in surprise. One by one, they muttered words of approval.

The captain's eyebrows rose. "Good work, son. Smart sailors have always looked to the stars for guidance. Get some sleep now, you've earned the right. I'll finish the watch. You're excused, lad, go to bed."

So Alan got into his bunk, happier than on any night since stowing away on the *Devora*. He was too excited to sleep. At last he had done something worthwhile on this ship! Too bad Rae hadn't been awake to see the whole business. She had actually smiled at him during tonight's lesson. Before this journey is over, he promised himself, I'll make her change her opinion of me altogether. Whatever it takes.

It seemed he had slept only a moment when he was awakened by a loud shout, "Sail ho! To the south!"

The scramble of crew members leaping from their bunks and running out on deck got him to his feet. Outside, it was daybreak. On the distant horizon Alan could just make out a ship with two triangular sails.

Saul's voice boomed out, "Weapons on the ready, men!" His next words froze the blood in Alan's veins. "It's an Arab raider!"

◇ CHAPTER SEVEN ◇

lan ran to the rail. The Arab pirate ship was still too far away to make out anything clearly. Next to him Rae was peering at the horizon, too.

"What's going to happen?" He hoped he didn't sound scared.

"There's going to be a fight, I know it!" She drew her scimitar and lunged at an imaginary enemy.

Alan retreated out of range. "Would your father let you fight?" None of the girls he knew in Toulon had anything to do with fighting.

"Why on earth not? He's the one that taught me!" She stuck out her chin.

He squinted at the oncoming ship. "What kind of sails

are those? I've never seen such shapes before." The sails were great triangles, not squares.

"Lateen sails, that's what the Arabs use." She gave him a sideways glance. "They told me what you did last night. Said you kept us from winding up in the harbor of Tripoli. Where did you learn so much about the stars?"

"From my father. He—"

Saul's voice broke in. "Come along, you two!" He put a hand on each of their shoulders and moved them away from the rail. "Into the fo'c'sle with you both, c'mon! Quick march!"

"No, Father, give me a chance!" Rae raised her voice in protest. "I want to stay and fight! You taught me how to use a scimitar, remember?" She stabbed the air again with her weapon. "I'm as good as any man!"

Alan pulled out his scimitar. "Why should I hide? I can fight if she can!"

Saul's eyebrows went up at this show of bravado. "Maybe next time. But not now! Get going!" He marched them over to the cabin and shoved them inside the door. "A good sailor obeys orders. Remember that, both of you. Stay inside. And no nonsense—this isn't a game we're playing!" He pulled the key from the inside lock and slammed the door shut. They heard the heavy bolt slide into place.

Alan sank onto a bench. "We're going to miss everything, stuck here." It was disappointing to be left out of the action, waiting in a stuffy cabin. And yet, he

was a bit relieved.

Rae stamped her foot. "It's not fair!" Then a smile spread over her face. Her finger pointed. "Look! Father forgot about the window. We don't have to miss a thing!"

Alan's eyes followed to where she was pointing. True, the window shutters did open from the inside. "But what about your father's orders?" All very well for her to disobey, she was Saul's daughter.

"Who wants to stay stuck in here?" Rae flung back at him. She was already halfway out the window.

Alan followed. It was only a short drop to the deck. Rae motioned for him to stay close to the fo'c'sle wall, where they could watch unseen. She grinned at him, and he grinned back. A surge of delight went through him. This is great, he thought, we're on the same side for once.

They watched the pirate ship swell in size as it came closer. The anxious muttering of the rowers grew louder. Everyone on deck was in motion.

Saul was shouting orders. "Ship oars! Reef the sail!" Three of the sailors swarmed up to the top yardarm and began to tie up the sail. Soon, the Arab ship put about and pulled alongside the *Devora*.

Alan's heart was racing. What was going to happen? If it came to hand-to-hand combat, the kind he'd practiced with Hugo, was he good enough to survive? This time it wouldn't be practice, but for real. Life or death. But he had never beaten Hugo. And he'd never even used the scimitar. Was he ready for real combat? What would

it feel like, to kill another human being?

He glanced sideways at Rae. Was she as bloodthirsty as she sounded? With that close-fitting blue cap pulled down over her forehead, she became a cabin boy again. Could she really fight a barbarous pirate? Maybe he should've talked her into staying in the cabin with him. If anything happened to her, it would be his fault.

"Say," he whispered to Rae, "why didn't the captain just use the rowers and try to get away?"

"A lot of good it would've done! Arab ships are faster, that's why. Besides, we Radanites never run away from anything!"

They peered around the corner of the cabin. The men of the *Devora*, with scimitars drawn, had formed a line on deck facing the Arab ship. Saul stood in front of them, one hand on the hilt of his scimitar.

Crash! Three large iron hooks tied to ropes came hurtling out of the pirate ship and thumped onto the deck of the *Devora*. The ropes were yanked taut until the hooks caught the railing. Now the two ships were bound together.

Rae sucked in her breath sharply. "This is it."

An agile figure vaulted over the rails and leaped onto their deck. A giant of a man, he was naked to the waist and dark of skin. Barefoot, he was clothed only in black pantaloons that reached from waist to knee. Twisted about his head was a turban of many colors. In his right hand he gripped a long, shining scimitar. The first rays

of the sun illuminated the deep scowl on his face. Almost instantly he was followed by half a dozen others, dressed and armed in the same way.

The pirates faced Captain Isaac and his men. The giant shouted something in a language Alan had never heard.

"What's he saying?" he whispered to Rae.

She whispered back, "It's Arabic. 'Christian dogs, surrender, or you'll all die!'" Alan shivered; he was a Christian.

Deliberately, with unhurried steps, Captain Isaac came forward and faced the intruder. About his shoulders was wrapped his white prayer shawl. The Radanite captain stood tall and imposing, with no weapon of any kind in his hand. "You are mistaken! We're not Christians! Observe the prayer shawl I'm wearing. We're People of the Book!" He spoke in Arabic.

The pirate seemed taken aback. He waved his scimitar at Isaac. "What are you doing in our waters?"

"A mistake. Our helmsman threw us off course." The captain stepped forward calmly until he stood directly in front of the pirate leader. While the giant watched, Isaac drew the top of his robe apart.

Alan poked Rae. "What's the captain doing?"

She shrugged. "Who knows?"

Peering, Alan could just make out a large golden medallion hanging from a chain around the captain's neck. Isaac held it up to the pirate's eyes. "Do you recognize this?"

The man bent forward. Then his head snapped back in surprise. "That's the sign of our caliph!"

The captain nodded. "You're right. This is a gift from His Majesty, Harun-al-Rashid himself. It gives us the right to pass through your waters. We're on a mission to Baghdad."

The pirate pointed his finger at Isaac. "How do I know you didn't steal this from a real friend of the caliph?"

The captain smiled and spoke again. The words that flowed from his lips were clear and ringing.

Rae whispered, "Something about Abraham...." Her brow wrinkled as she tried to grasp what was going on.

When Isaac finished, he and the pirate chief stood silent for a moment. The only sounds were those of the waves slapping against the sides of the vessels and the occasional bump of the pirate ship against the *Devora.* The sun's rays glinted on the curved scimitars.

The giant shifted from one foot to the other, his brow furrowed. The men behind him moved restlessly, fingering the hilts of their weapons. Saul and the sailors of the *Devora* stayed motionless, eyeing the two leaders. The sun moved higher in the sky.

Watching, Alan felt as though he could hardly breathe.

The captain broke the silence. "In our cargo are many handsome gifts. From our king to His Majesty Harun-al-Rashid."

"Ah!" The pirate's eyebrows rose. He nodded vigorously, his lips opened in a broad smile. "Go with

the blessings of Allah!" He thrust his scimitar back into his belt and bowed to Isaac. The captain returned the bow. At a command, the pirate crew sheathed their weapons. Quickly they unhooked their ship from the *Devora* and sprang back over the rails. The Radanites put away their scimitars. A few moments later, the ship with the lateen sails was moving away to the south. Saul shouted an order. The drum beat began, and the rowers bent to their task.

Smiling, the Radanites looked at each other. "Say," shouted one of the crew, "the captain won without a fight!" Jubilant, they surrounded Isaac, offering congratulations. Two of the sailors hooked their arms together and stomped out a jig on deck while the others beat time with their hands. Alan and Rae sidled out of their hiding place in a hurry to join the celebration. They ran right into Saul.

"You two?" His stern look went from one to the other, as he stood with his arms folded. "I gave you orders to stay in the fo'c'sle till I unlocked the door!"

"Don't be such a spoilsport, Father." Rae's voice was silken. "We couldn't stay locked up like babies, we just couldn't. We had to know what was going on. What if you'd needed help?" She reached out and put a hand on her father's arm. "Besides, the window was open."

"I ought to put you both on bread and water for disobeying orders!" Saul snapped. "Alan, you should have known better! I'm disappointed in you." He turned

to Rae. "You're a crew member, too. You've got to obey orders like anyone else." He pursed his lips. "See that it never happens again! Rae, you're excused for now. I want to talk to Alan."

She gave them a curious glance and hurried off to join the other sailors who were still singing and dancing, celebrating their escape.

"Tell, me, Alan, what if today had ended in a real fight? You would've been drawn into it, believe me. How well can you use that scimitar of yours?"

Alan hesitated. His mind played back the scene of Hugo slashing murderously away with his sword, and driving Alan, cowering, back against the wall. His father's face was grim at the sight of his son making a fool of himself. Should he tell Saul the truth?

In the glare reflected from the sea, he couldn't bear to lie. "I've never used my scimitar in a real battle. Not yet."

"Never fought with it, eh?" Saul tapped the hilt of Alan's scimitar. "Let's have a look at it." Alan drew the scimitar from its sheath and handed it to him. Saul whistled. "Hmmm, a fine blade. Where did you get it?"

"A present from my father. Souvenir of the war against the Moors."

Saul grunted. "But you've never used it."

"I've had lessons—" Alan hesitated. "With the long sword."

"Long sword?" Saul's lips curled in amusement.

"Hacking and chopping? A lot of good that'll do you around here! On a ship there's not much space. And not a second to waste, with pirates vaulting over the walls. Today we were lucky, tomorrow who knows?" He shrugged.

"Well, I can learn, can't I?"

"You'd better!" Saul handed back Alan's weapon. "Look, Jason's one of our best swordsmen. I'll arrange for him to give you some real practice. You'll have to get used to it. Life on the trade routes is full of danger, you saw what went on today. If ours had been a Christian ship, you know what would've happened?"

Alan raised his eyebrows. Without speaking, Saul slid a finger across his throat. Just then Isaac joined them, and Saul mentioned the upcoming scimitar lessons. The captain agreed: the lessons should begin without delay.

When Saul went aft to check the helm, Alan said, "Captain, I was impressed by the way you dealt with those pirates. But tell me. What did you say to the pirate that made him change his mind?"

Isaac smiled. "Well, first I told him we were the People of the Book."

"Oh, Rae translated that. But she didn't get the last part. Something about Abraham—?"

The captain's smile deepened. "Oh, that. I just quoted a few lines from their Holy Book, the Koran. 'Who except the foolish would reject the religion of Abraham? We have surely chosen him in the world.' And then I

reminded him that we Radanites are children of Abraham, too."

Alan was surprised. "So the Arabs' religion is the same as yours?"

Isaac shook his head. "Judaism existed long before the prophet Mohammed had his vision. Our faith is over two thousand years old! And Islam, less than two hundred. But their prophet borrowed some of our basic ideas when he started Islam on its way."

"And my church—the Christians—we use your Old Testament, too!"

The captain nodded. "That's right, the same one. We all have a lot in common. So isn't it strange that there's so little peace among us?" His gaze went past Alan out to the horizon. "Well, we should be getting under way." He wet a finger and held it up. "Ah, the wind has freshened. Why don't you see if Saul is getting ready to drop the sail?"

When Alan got to the mast, Saul had just given the order. Jason was already climbing toward the top yardarm. Alan stared upward, remembering his first try. Suddenly he was disgusted with himself. If all the others could do it, why shouldn't he? Anything was better than standing around feeling helpless. Without hesitating, he sprang to the ladder and began to climb. This time he didn't look down. He just kept going, arm over arm, step after step, following Jason.

Jason's grinning face peered at him as he neared the

top yardarm. "Well, look who's here! We'll make a seaman of you yet!"

Alan squirmed over to the side to make room for the next man and untied one of the ropes holding the reefed sail. When the final knot was undone, the sail fell. As the bottom was secured, the great white square billowed out in the wind. He felt like whooping aloud. He'd made it—he was on top of the world!

But going down was a lot scarier than going up. He waited until the others were gone and then climbed slowly all the way down. He smiled to himself because he hadn't gotten dizzy this time. And he was still alive, standing firmly on the deck. He could do it the same as Rae, though maybe not quite as fast yet. Still, it was a victory.

Jason was watching for him at the foot of the mast. "Saul asked me about giving you scimitar lessons. Well, there's no duty for us for a bit. How about right now?"

Alan shrugged. "Why not?" He glanced about to see if Rae was watching, but there was no sign of her. Saul and the captain had disappeared, too. All the others were occupied, so he and Jason were quite alone. Thank God, only Jason would find out how bad he was at swordplay.

Jason drew his scimitar and motioned for Alan to do the same. "All right. Make believe I'm a pirate. You'd better move fast. So, attack!"

"Watch out—" Alan gritted his teeth and made a couple of wild swings. Jason dodged them easily by just stepping aside.

"Slow down!" Jason stared at him. "Where in the name of heaven did you learn to attack like that?"

Alan reddened. "Well, the only swordplay I've ever had was with a long sword."

Jason hooted. "You mean that heavy piece of steel that you have to grip with both hands and swing like you're chopping wood?" He rolled his eyes upward. "No wonder! Look, Alan, a scimitar's a completely different kind of weapon. You don't just hack away, hoping to make minced meat out of your opponent."

"I was taught that was the idea," Alan said stiffly.

"I'm glad you didn't have to fight one of those pirates today with that technique! By the time you finished your first swing, he would've run you through!" Jason guffawed. "What did you do in that castle of yours, Count Alan, sit around on a throne and give orders?"

"You don't know anything, Jason!" Alan drew himself up and found, to his great satisfaction, that he was actually taller than Jason. "My father won honors fighting the Moors for our king. Anyway, counts don't sit on thrones."

"Oh?" Jason looked him up and down. "You're not much for muscles, that's for sure. Tall, though, that's a help. Don't worry, muscles don't count as much as skill in this kind of fighting. Actually, it's more of an art. You should see how good at it even a little thing like Rae is!"

Alan stared. "How did she get that way? You mean she's been in hand-to-hand combat?" Was there anything

Rae couldn't do?

Jason shrugged. "Her father taught her. Fact is, if you don't know how to defend yourself, you won't last long around here."

"But he locked us both in the fo'c'sle!"

"Naturally, he's a father. And you were untested. No use taking chances. By the way—" He frowned. "Just because you're getting to spend a lot of time with Rae on those lessons, don't get any ideas."

"Ideas? What do you mean?"

"I've heard plenty of stories. About how you noblemen take advantage of girls."

"Are you crazy? Do you think the lessons were my idea? As far as I'm concerned, Rae is just a cabin boy!" He eyed Jason. "Besides, what business is it of yours?"

An unmistakable flush darkened Jason's tanned face, outlining the scar on his cheek. "Never mind. Let's get started."

Was there something between Jason and Rae, Alan wondered, as he lifted his scimitar. Who cared, anyway? He had more important things to worry about. Only he knew how desperately he needed Jason's lessons. Because whether he was tracing letters painstakingly with Rae or pulling with all his might on the steering oar, one picture never left the back of his mind.

The shadowy figure of Cousin Hugo.

◇ CHAPTER EIGHT ◇

Constantinople!" exclaimed Samuel, pushing aside his empty bowl. "You haven't lived till you've seen it!"

"You're right!" The little cook, Moises, rolled his eyes. "Makes London and Paris look like mud villages!"

"I can't wait!" For days Alan had heard tales about Constantinople, the capital city of Byzantium. The Radanite sailors raved over the gold and jewels decorating the palaces and churches. Now, after weeks at sea, everyone was waiting patiently for a glimpse of the glories.

But all Alan would get to see was the waterfront, the part of the city called the Golden Horn. They were behind schedule, Saul explained to the crew, because of Samuel's

falling asleep at the helm. Only a small party would go ashore for enough supplies to take them to Trebizond. Everyone else had to stay on board.

Alan felt sorry for freckle-faced Samuel, with everyone blaming him. The crew grumbled openly. It was a bitter disappointment. To be so near the splendors of Constantinople without a chance to see them firsthand!

The *Devora* crossed the Sea of Marmara and approached the Golden Horn. Alan ran to the rail with the others for the first glimpse of the domes and minarets. After he had drunk in the sight for a while, he sought out Saul.

"Here!" He held out his purse. "For the extra rations you needed for me."

The bos'n pushed Alan's hand back. "No need, boy. Captain's orders. You're earning your keep."

By the time they reached Byzantium, Alan's reading and writing had improved so much that Rae had begun teaching him Arabic. "When we get to Baghdad you'd look ignorant if you didn't understand it."

After the pirate ship episode, Alan had expected the classes to be different. But Rae was Rae. She made it plain that they were teacher and pupil. Everything during class was strictly business. As for Jason, Alan noticed that lately he seemed to be hanging around whenever a lesson ended. Was he jealous?

The lessons with Jason continued as well. Though the early scimitar lessons left Alan with muscles that protested, Jason never seemed to tire. This morning, with the

Devora lying motionless at the dock, was no exception.

"All right, once more. Scimitar in the on-guard position! Good. Now thrust! No, no, not like that! This isn't a stick you're playing soldier with! It's a curved scimitar. Curved, understand? Your thrust has to be upward, so your enemy will get the point!" Jason roared at his own joke.

Alan braced himself for another attack. As he lunged forward, a strange thing happened. Jason's sunburned face took on the long contours of Hugo's with its aquiline nose. All the blood in Alan's body came to a boil. One thing mattered more than anything in the world. To blot out Hugo's mocking smile forever. To run his scimitar through Hugo and watch his body crumple at his feet!

After parrying a few of Alan's wild swings, Jason caught Alan's blade with his own. With a sharp twist, he wrenched the weapon out of Alan's hand. The scimitar struck the deck with a loud clang. "Take it easy!" Jason shouted. "What's wrong with you?"

Alan stood transfixed and stared at the face that had now become Jason's. What had he been thinking of? Had he been trying to kill him? Breathing hard, he bent and picked up his scimitar. "I—uh—I'm sorry. Don't know what got into me."

Jason bit his lip. "Watch yourself!" He motioned with his weapon. "Let's start again. On-guard position. Only with control this time, right? You can't control others till you can control yourself. Now, attack!"

But Alan found it hard to forgive himself. How had he let his rage against Hugo blot out reality? What if he had wounded Jason? The lesson went badly.

"Enough for one day, let's quit," Jason said finally. Alan was relieved to sheath his scimitar.

The day dragged on, warm and humid. A faint fragrance of spices mingled with the stench of rotting fruit. Everyone was grumpy, waiting for the supplies to be brought back on board. The bustle of the city was only a gangplank's length away, but they couldn't leave the ship. Whoever heard of such a thing? Being in an exotic port and not even allowed to set foot there!

Leaning at the rail, Alan fought a nagging worry. Would he ever be able to fight as well as Jason? Otherwise, how could he outwit Hugo? Suddenly he wished with all his heart that he was back at the castle, laughing with his fair-haired mother over his dog Brunhilde's newest trick. He could almost feel the soft fur of Brunhilde's neck and hear the welcoming rumble as she rubbed her muzzle into his hand.

How was his mother faring? His mother, who had managed to put aside her private grief to comfort him after the accident. She'd pushed the cloud of hair back from her forehead and drawn him down onto the bench next to her. "Alan, you've got to stop feeling guilty. Your father's death wasn't your fault—don't blame yourself! Don't you see, there was nothing anyone could've done." She'd held him and they'd wept together.

If only he could catch a glimpse of the castle and the tangled green of the forest behind it! And his mother. How lighthearted she used to be, flying out the door to greet his father and fall into his arms laughing.

Despair made everything around him hideous, from the heavy, sticky air to the hubbub of the passersby on the wharf. I'm sharing quarters with a crew, he thought, but not one of them really cares whether I live or die. If anything, they usually laugh at me. Jason, Saul, Rae, everybody. Well, maybe not Moises. What am I doing aboard this hostile ship?

A burst of noise and laughter signaled the return of the shore party. They were using some of the rowers to carry the sacks and barrels of food and drink. Alan tried to shut out their chatter about the sights in the marketplace. He had never been so homesick in his life.

Early in the morning, the oars moved the *Devora* out into the rising tide and through the narrow channel that connected the Sea of Marmara with the Black Sea. The crew had plenty to do. Alan found it a relief to be kept busy.

The *Devora* was heading southeast toward Trebizond, the kingdom on the Black Sea's southern shore. Their first night on the sea fell on a Friday, a clear evening, with a sky made bright by the full moon. Alan took the helm so that all of the crew members could go through the Radanite rituals of blessings and wine-sippings. Then he returned to the cabin, where Moises fed him a tasty

supper of roasted fowl, fresh melon, and pomegranates bought in the markets of Constantinople. Afterward the crew, except for helmsman and lookout, gathered in a circle on the deck. A lively breeze filled the sail, giving the rowers some rest.

"Listen, Captain," said a crewman, "you promised us a look at Empress Irene's palace. But we never got anywhere near it!"

"I know, I know—my apologies."

"But you've been there before, haven't you?"

Isaac nodded.

"Captain, is it true she has golden lions that roar?" Rae asked.

Isaac smiled. "That's one place you don't forget."

A chorus rose. "Come on, Captain, tell us about it!"

"Well, Rachel's right, she does have golden lions. In the Great Hall of the palace. The ceiling of the hall is a deep blue dome with twinkling yellow and white stars."

"And the lions?" Rae asked, leaning forward.

"Ah, those lions! Their manes bristle and their mouths are open. One sits on each side of the gold-and-ivory throne. And next to each lion is a huge silver birdcage on a ten-foot-tall column." Isaac stretched his hand high above his head. "In each cage you see a small tree with golden branches. And on each tree sit five golden birds!"

"Ooh." Rae hugged herself, her eyes glittered. "All that gold and silver."

Samuel shook his head. "Imagine, ten golden birds.

Each worth a fortune!" His brow wrinkled. "Say, Captain, what are the women of Byzantium like?"

Everybody laughed. Isaac spread his hands wide. "You've never seen such gowns. A parade of splendor! Rubies, emeralds, diamonds flashing everywhere. Scarves of gold and silver threads. The men in tunics of white silk. Only in Byzantium!"

"What about the empress herself?"

"Irene? A tiny thing, but you should see the crown she wears. Heavy with jewels!"

Alan leaned forward. In his mind floated a vision of the great throne room, the array of dazzling women drifting by in their glitter. He could almost smell their Eastern perfumes and hear the rustle of their silks. "But Captain, what about the emperor? Isn't he there?" Alan asked.

"Irene's husband? Of course, Leo was emperor of Byzantium. But they say she poisoned both him and his father! Just to get the throne for herself."

A murmur went around the group. "Talk about ambition—" Jason said, half to himself.

Alan shuddered at the tale. Like his cousin Hugo, who was waiting to kill him. Just to get his hands on the castle and the lands. The same greed and lust for power. Suddenly he was ashamed of how badly the scimitar lesson had gone. And how he had sulked and grown homesick just because he couldn't go ashore.

How would he ever get the best of Hugo if he didn't discard such childish habits?

◇ CHAPTER NINE ◇

The captain was speaking. "So the empress is seated and the show begins. A great roar comes from the lions. You'd swear they were alive! Then the golden birds begin singing."

Samuel whistled. "Amazing!"

"Wait! Slowly the throne, with Irene on it, rises right up in the air. And when it stops, she's sitting three cubits above everyone's head!" Again he stretched his long arm straight up.

Jason frowned. "How do they do that, Captain? Not black magic, is it?"

Isaac shook his head. "No magic to it. Just science. The Greeks learned how to do it long ago. It works by

getting a column of water to balance with a column of air. The air pushes on the water, and the water raises the throne. Simple engineering. The sound of the lions and the birds is made by forcing air out of pipes."

There was a moment of silence. Alan pictured a golden throne bearing an empress high in the air. He could hear the melodious piping of the golden birds and the terrifying roar of the golden lions. "Constantinople must be far ahead of Marseilles."

"No question! That's why they say, 'Out of the East came the light.'" Captain Isaac stood up. "Time to change the watch."

It was Alan's watch. He went forward and gazed out over the shining path that streaked from the moon across the dark waters to the *Devora*. A snatch of song floated out of the fo'c'sle. Now and then a whiff of smoking food drifted from the galley to his nostrils. Maybe life aboard a ship wasn't so bad, after all. Tonight, for example, he'd felt a part of a charmed circle, sitting with his shipmates under the open sky, listening to the captain's yarn. Someday he'd come back to Byzantium and see that fairy-tale palace.

Soon after, the *Devora* headed south for Trebizond, and the spell of fine weather vanished. On the third day out, the sun was extinguished by black clouds that rolled in from the east. The wind picked up and the ship began to pitch as the waves rose higher.

Alan, who had been asleep below following his watch,

was awakened by a volley of shouts mingled with frantic screams. A sudden lurch of the ship nearly threw him out of his bunk. He ran up on deck in time to see the clouds split by a blinding streak of lightning. A crash of thunder followed. Drops of icy rain smashed onto the deck like hailstones. Saul was everywhere at once, shouting orders. Alan realized the screams were coming from below. The shackled slaves sounded terrified.

"Keep 'er into the wind!" Saul was yelling at the helmsman and his helper, who were both leaning into the steering oar. "Don't let 'er get broadside!" To the crew members who hurried forward he cried, "Reef the sail! Quick now!"

Three of the Radanites swarmed up to the yardarm, while the others hauled on the ropes tied to the sail's bottom. Watching, Alan marveled that the three could keep their balance and manage to tie up the sail at the same time.

What could he do? Should he climb the ladder and help them? But it was all he could do to keep his footing on the pitching deck. Besides, it only took the three a few moments to do their job. They slid back down and ran to obey other orders Saul was flinging at them.

Rae came rushing out of the cabin and almost bumped into Alan. "Why are you standing there doing nothing?" Before he could answer that no one had told him what to do, she glanced up. "Look! The sail!"

Alan squinted upward through the rain that was now

lashing the deck in torrents. The knot of one of the ropes used to reef the sail had become undone. That corner was now loose and flapping in the wind. Before he could stop her, Rae shouted, "I'll get it!" and bounded up the ladder.

Saul caught sight of what was happening and ran to the foot of the mast. "Rachel," he shouted, "you hear me? Rachel? Come down!"

The troughs of the waves had deepened and the roll of the ship increased. Rae was being swung back and forth on her perilous perch. Without thinking, Alan grabbed hold of the ladder and began to pull himself up toward Rae. But only a little way up, the swaying of the mast made him dizzy. He stopped and looked up.

Rae had managed to get to the yardarm, grasp the loose rope, and retie it. Then she started down toward where Alan was hanging on for dear life. As he watched her, a downward lurch of the *Devora* made Rae lose her grip on the ladder. To Alan's horror, she began slipping. He twisted his body around in a frantic effort to break her fall.

But Rae's hand shot out and grasped one of the ropes holding the mast. In the next moment, she managed to grab it with her other hand and slide down. Alan gave a sigh of relief and started down the ladder.

Suddenly a great wave broke and slapped the bow of the *Devora* downward. Rae was flung from the line to the deck, where she lay in a motionless heap.

Just as Alan leaped from the bottom of the ladder to

get to her, another gigantic wave cascaded over the deck. The force of the water washed Rae toward the rail. Alan found himself knocked flat, too, away from her. Somehow he managed to stretch out one hand. He caught hold of Rae's foot.

But it wasn't enough. Another wave followed, washing them both closer to the rail. He clung to her foot desperately. Before they reached the edge of the deck he'd have to get a better grip on her. How could he do it? The *Devora* rolled, and the two of them slid the other way in a great wash of foaming water. It was impossible for him to see where they were headed.

A roaring filled his ears. Was that Saul screaming at him? Alan tried to shout back. Salty water filled his mouth. A silent prayer began in his head. He was alone with Rae in a cold, green underworld.

Together they were sliding into the raging sea.

◇ CHAPTER TEN ◇

The sea was his enemy. It sucked him forward and hurled him back.

He struggled to breathe as the foaming water cascaded over him. Somehow he was still hanging on to Rae's ankle. His fingers were grateful for the grittiness of her wet hose. Bare skin would have been impossible—she would have slipped away.

Had their sliding stopped? Alan opened his eyes and saw two sturdy legs planted on either side of him. Strong hands were reaching down to grasp his shoulders. As he sat up, he could see Rae being lifted—her body looked limp. In a moment the captain had dragged him away from the edge of the deck. The next thing Alan knew,

he was in his bunk. His soaked clothes were being pulled off and a dry blanket was being wrapped around him. He couldn't stop shivering; he was cold through and through.

"Better take it easy for a bit, lad." Isaac tucked the blanket under his icy feet. Alan muttered his thanks as the captain left.

It felt good just to lie there in the swaying hammock. The rough wool blanket was scratchy but thick. Little by little the numb chill left his hands and feet. Finally a sensation of warmth spread all through him, as blissful as spring sunshine. In spite of the howling of the wind outside and the violent pitching of the *Devora*, he became drowsy and closed his eyes.

He woke in a panic. What was wrong? How long had he slept? The ship was rocking, so the storm was still out there. A dream had possessed him, a dream that Rae had slid from his grasp. He was swimming, trying to reach her, but the waves were mountainous. She was being tossed farther and farther out to sea.

Sweating, he sat bolt upright and wiped his forehead with the back of his hand. The terror of the dream persisted. What about Rae? Was she all right?

He jumped up, pulled on a dry tunic and britches, and dashed outside. By this time, the wind and rain had begun to slacken. A thin line of blue was edging the eastern horizon. The waves had settled down to a steady chop. Saul was shouting for the rowers to begin. "Start the drum! Unfurl the sail! You two, go below and see

to the slaves! Lively, now!"

Alan spotted Isaac and went over to him. "Captain, how's Rachel? Is she badly hurt?"

The captain took his eyes away from the activity aloft. "Don't worry. Rachel's in good shape, and we're glad you are, too." Then his eyes went past Alan and he frowned. "Rachel? Shouldn't you be in bed?"

Alan turned. Rae stood there, her damp red curls encircled by a cloth bandage. "You're hurt!" he exclaimed.

She shook her head. "Just a nasty bump." She came right up to him. Her skin looked very pale, as if the sea had scoured her. A scent of some pungent herb clung to her, medicine rubbed on the bruise. Her eyes searched his face. "Saul told me what you did. I owe you my life, Alan."

Was that what a mermaid looked like, with milky skin and gray-green eyes? He stood enjoying her smile. "Luckily I was too scared to go all the way up the ladder."

"Scared? But you weren't too scared to hang on to me." She gave Alan a quick hug. Over her shoulder, he spotted Jason watching them from the helm.

Rae hugging him! Would wonders never cease? Alan felt his face flush, and his heart soared like a hawk on the wind. He put his arms around her and hugged her back. Who cared if everyone was watching! "That? It was easy—"

She stepped back, her expression changed. She frowned in the old familiar way. "But, you idiot, why on earth

did you try to climb the mast? You haven't had enough practice! Besides, I had the knot all tied. Don't you know you could've been killed!" With a sniff, she whirled about and stamped her way back to the cabin.

Alan's jaw dropped. What had he done wrong?

A hand fell on his shoulder, it was the bos'n. "Never mind Rachel—you know how girls are. Who can figure them out? She shouldn't have climbed the mast herself, either. Alan, you have a father's thanks for saving her life."

The captain gave Alan an approving nod. His shipmates came by and clapped Alan on the back. "That took a lot of pluck, kid, you did all right," Moises said.

The truth was, it had all happened so fast that Alan hadn't had time to think. Was that what courage was?

All he wanted now was to relish the perfect surprise of Rae's hug. True, it had been a bit spoiled by her sudden flash of anger. And he had had another surprise—Jason's dark glance. Why had Jason looked so angry watching them? Was there an understanding between him and Rae? Back in Toulon, marriages were arranged by families long before children grew up. He smiled to think that now Jason was jealous of him, the newcomer.

Wait a minute. Was that why Saul interrupted our lesson that night? Doesn't he trust me alone with Rae? Is he worried that I might interfere with a set arrangement? There's only one thing that matters. How does Rae feel about Jason?

Anyway, she did hug me. Even if she did go away mad. But I've got to face the fact that Jason's five years older. And a skilled swordsman. Besides, he's one of her own kind. Do I even stand a chance?

But what am I dreaming about? I've got all I can do to get ready for the day I can take on Hugo. If I lose my head over Rae, it could wreck everything. I made a vow on my father's grave. And that's going to take all my attention to live up to.

"Hey, slowpoke!" Rae's head popping out of the cabin door interrupted his thoughts. "What're you doing, daydreaming? It's lesson time! Today's no holiday!"

Alan gave a mock sigh. On the *Devora*, it seemed, school was never out. Rae was as stern a taskmaster as ever. But that hug had changed everything. Her armor had been pierced.

A week later, the rowers edged the *Devora* next to one of the wharves at the waterfront of Trebizond on the south shore of the Black Sea. The town was a big, lively trading center, filled with people from the four corners of the earth.

Stepping off the gangplank, Alan found it hard to keep his balance at first. "Take it slow, lad. You've got to get your land legs back," said Moises, holding out a steadying arm.

Almost at once, Alan was immersed in a babble of different languages. Soldiers, seamen, beggars, and well-dressed merchants in flowing robes jostled each other,

talking or arguing. He found himself having to step aside nimbly for elegant palanquins carried on the shoulders of bearers. And his very life was threatened by drivers of horse-drawn carts, waving their whips and shouting in Arabic, "Make way! Make way!"

The slight breeze from the water did not really cool the air, which was sultry at midday. A spicy aroma drifted from the stalls of vendors, who offered pieces of roast fowl or chunks of fat mutton on long skewers. In front of some of the shops were baskets of odd-shaped fruits, green and yellow and orange, that Alan had never seen before.

Beggars thrust their hands into his face, crying, "*Baksheesh!* Alms, for the love of God!" Ragged children pulled at his tunic, wheedling in several languages. The few Arabic words he caught promised to show him the sights of the city for a few coins. The noise beat in his ears.

On the wharf next to the *Devora*, the captain was bargaining with a group of traders. Alan watched as they frowned and waved their hands about. Finally, with nods and smiles, they shook hands all around. The slaves were herded down the gangplank and onto the dock, where they were soon marched away by the traders.

"Are they buying our whole cargo, Captain?" Alan asked.

Isaac nodded. "Yes, good business all around. We'll get everything we need for our caravan."

"Clothing, too?"

"The whole works, lad. Food, garments, animals, and tents. Even guides."

Alan prayed he wouldn't be among those left behind in Trebizond. "Won't some of the crew have to stay here to take care of the ship?"

Isaac was watching the parade of Saxon slaves following their new masters. "Of course. Most of them, in fact. There'll be plenty to do, keeping the *Devora* in trim. A neglected ship soon rots."

"Then who'll be going to Baghdad, Captain?" The crew had been speculating about who'd be picked. Alan could hardly wait for the answer. Visions of the fabled city of Baghdad had been floating into his dreams lately. But he was the last of the crew to join. And a stowaway, to boot. So he hadn't even asked.

The captain stroked his beard. "Travel by caravan is a risky business. And very expensive." He studied Alan's face. "Hard choices. You, now, perhaps you'd be better off snug and safe on the *Devora*—"

"And miss Baghdad? But, Captain, that's what I want to see more than anything in the world!"

Isaac looked pleased. "That's what I wanted to hear. Well, lad, the day you saved Saul's daughter you earned the right to come with us. Besides, you've worked hard and learned fast. Then it's settled. We'll only be a small group: Saul, Jason, Rachel, you, and I."

"I can hardly wait!" Gold-tipped minarets floated in his head.

"Mind you, it's not child's play. Always danger from roaming bandits. And the desert sun never gives up trying to burn you to a cinder." He eyed Alan. "Still want to come?"

"Oh, yes, Captain, I'll take my chances! When do we leave?" He was really going!

"With luck, this very day, if the guides show up soon and we get all the supplies packed on the donkeys. There's no time to lose. We need to cross the desert before the hottest days of summer arrive. Well, better get your things together."

Alan felt like climbing the mast and shouting out the good news. Baghdad! I'm one of the lucky ones, I'm going! Even my father never traveled so far! If only I could tell Mother. It's hard not to worry about what her days are like. How is that vile Hugo treating her?

Hugo. Probably busy raising an army right now. Will I be tough enough by the time I get back from this mission to have it out with him? At least I'm growing taller, I can tell from my clothes. And my muscles are strong enough now to handle the steering oar. Anyway, there's still plenty of time to worry about Hugo.

Right now only one thing matters. I'm going to Baghdad with Rae!

◇ CHAPTER ELEVEN ◇

Going back up the gangplank to the deck, Alan found Rae standing at the rail watching the crowds. "Guess what, I'm going with the caravan, too!" Would she be glad?

"You mean you didn't ask until now?"

So she knew before he did. No matter, he was learning to dodge Rae's darts. "Does the desert begin on the other side of the city?"

"Don't you know any geography? We don't get to the desert for weeks! First we have to cross the mountains of Pontus and Armenia."

Alan sighed. She knew everything. "So we use horses, right?"

"For the mountains, yes. But when we get to the desert, we switch to camels."

Camels? Father Paulus had once taken him to the abbey in Toulon. There, the priest had shown him a large book called a bestiary. Because books were as rare as gold, it was chained to a desk for safekeeping. On one page was a drawing of a camel. Alan recalled the amazing creature with its long neck and high-humped back. But he had never expected to see one.

The whole idea of going to Baghdad excited him tremendously. But Rae was acting as though making the trip was as ordinary as shopping at the local marketplace. Naturally, she'd known all along that she'd be going with her father. Not only did she know Arabic, but she'd also made the trip once before.

The captain came hurrying on board. "We'll be under way within the hour!"

A sailor following him dumped a large bundle on the deck. Untied, it turned out to be a collection of hot-weather garments for the desert part of the trip. It didn't take long for Alan and the others to gather their things and stuff them into their packs. Meanwhile, the traders had returned with a string of ten horses and eight donkeys.

Everyone pitched in to help load supplies on the donkey's backs. The remaining donkeys carried the trading goods and gifts bound for Baghdad. When the loading was finished, Captain Isaac called out, "All right, men, a minute for farewells!" The Radanites exchanged

embraces.

"Shalom! May God go with you!" cried those staying behind. The travelers echoed, "Shalom!"

The Arab horses proved to be sleek and graceful, far different from the great clumsy destriers that knights rode in Toulon. Seated on a handsome chestnut mare, Alan tried not to show how excited he was. How lucky not to be with the group waving good-bye from the deck of the *Devora*!

He turned toward Jason, who was mounted next to him. "What are the other five horses for?"

"Horses get tired on tough mountain roads." Jason leaned forward to adjust his own horse's bridle. "Every so often, we'll be able to switch."

Three mounted Arabs rode up to the group and spoke to Isaac. Rae, riding on Alan's other side, pushed a curl under her cap. "They're our guides. The leader's name is Mahmud."

The captain lined up the caravan. He and Mahmud in front, Jason and Saul next, and Rae and Alan last. Behind them was the second guide, leading the five spare horses. Farther back, the third guide led the pack donkeys. Slowly, the train wound its way out to the southern edge of Trebizond.

Just beyond the city walls, six Arabs armed with bows as well as scimitars faced them on horseback. Their figures were dark and menacing against the sunlight.

Alarmed, Alan turned to Rae. "What do they want?"

She grinned. "Look pretty tough, don't they? Must be the soldiers to guard us. That's wild country out there. Never know who you'll run into."

Ahead, Alan could just make out the pale shapes of the mountains crouched on the horizon. He was used to the hills around Toulon and the cliffs near the sea. But he had never seen such lofty, jagged crests as those that lay ahead, purple against the sky. As they followed Mahmud, Alan realized that the path had already begun to wind gradually upward.

It was a relief to leave the noise of the city behind and ride under a canopy of green leaves. The only sounds were the shrill calls of birds and the buzz of insects, punctuated by the clip-clop of the horses' hooves. Far away, some dogs were barking. Alan noticed that he didn't have to guide his horse. The animal picked her way carefully as the path grew stonier. His mare seemed to know this region by heart.

At times, when the path was only wide enough for one, Rae rode in front of him. She rode as well as any man and probably better than many. A good thing that at least he was used to horses. But it jolted him that often, when they lined up again, Jason somehow managed to be riding next to Rae. It wasn't much fun to ride alone behind them, watching their heads turning toward each other as they chatted.

When the sun became a red plate dropping toward the western horizon, Mahmud called a halt. The caravan had

made its way well up into the foothills. Everyone pitched in setting up camp. Two of the guides did the cooking, and Alan had his first taste of Arab food.

First came a kind of stew that was so tasty that he wiped his wooden bowl clean with chunks of flat Arab bread. When, in halting Arabic, he asked Mahmud what was in the stew, Rae translated the answer. The stew was mag-huma, a spicy mixture of lamb, onions, and eggplant. For dessert, Mahmud served little sweet, sticky balls called hais, full of dates and almonds.

Day after day, the procession wound its way through the mountain passes. Sometimes they were up so high that Alan shivered in the sharp, cold wind that blew around the bare rocks. When the path dropped lower, the horses moved past evergreen trees and bushes.

Late one afternoon, the descending path led them to a lush valley on either side of a wide river. Mahmud pointed a finger. "The Tigris. Now we follow it straight to Baghdad!"

Some days later, Alan got his first sight of the desert. The desert resembled the sea, except that the green swells of water were replaced by endless waves of brown sand.

"It's tough going for the horses," Alan said to Rae, as his mare plowed through the soft sand.

"But we're almost there. We switch to camels at the oasis."

"Oasis?"

"It's a watering place in the desert, where you can stop

and rest. You'll see." She squinted. "Look over there—palm trees."

The trees against the horizon were unlike any that Alan had ever seen. Masses of feathery fronds on top of tall skinny trunks drooped out in all directions. Of course, none of this was new to Rae. Alan sighed. It wasn't easy to travel with her. Would she always be the know-it-all and he the wide-eyed ignoramus?

At the oasis, Alan saw live camels for the first time. Big and ungainly, the beasts had strange humps and long necks. Their lips curled upward, showing dangerous-looking teeth. Loud grunts issued from their throats.

The two new guides made all the camels kneel down. Supplies and gift packages were transferred from the donkeys. Two of the earlier guides headed back to Trebizond with the horses and donkeys.

Once the water casks were refilled, Saul called, "Let's mount up!"

Alan wasn't quite sure how to get onto the saddle of his camel. He waited to see what the others did. Catching his eye, Jason grinned. "It's easy, Alan. Watch!" With practiced grace, he vaulted up. Alan jumped the same way, but his right leg didn't quite make it. He was surprised to find himself sitting on the sand.

His camel turned its head and suddenly spat in his direction. Alan leaped aside too late. A big wet stain darkened his tunic. He scrubbed at it with a handful of sand. Rae's laughter made him red-faced and determined.

Jason guffawed. "Sorry, I forgot to warn you about camels, they have this nasty habit."

Alan gritted his teeth. His next leap brought him right onto the saddle. Before he knew it, his camel had risen and he found himself high in the air and somewhat breathless.

Riding a camel, he soon learned, was a lot harder than riding a horse. Not only was he twice as high off the ground, but also the motion was different. As the camel walked, the hump on which he sat holding the reins swayed back and forth. It was worse than the deck of the *Devora* in midsea.

"Isn't this fun?" Rae called out. She giggled, her cheeks pink.

"Terrific!" Alan decided right then and there that the motion wasn't going to bother him. "You get a great view up this high!"

After three days on his camel's back, he wished they could have sailed down the Tigris instead. But he soon learned how to make his camel kneel, in order to get up or down. And he found that camels, like horses, become friendly if a rider slips them a bit of food now and then. His camel actually stopped spitting at him.

The Tigris turned out to be far from straight. The river meandered, with endless twists and turns. Some of the bends in the river were so large that the guides cut across the sands to save time, rather than following along the banks. Suddenly, during such a crossing, Mahmud

stopped his camel and threw up one hand, the signal to halt. Isaac and Saul galloped over, puffs of sand swirling up from the camels' hooves.

Alan moved his camel beside Rae's. "What's the matter?"

"Who knows?" She leaned forward, squinting. "This place isn't paradise, you know. Lots of wild tribes and cutthroats. Something's up."

"Here comes your father."

Saul's camel raced down the line. "Trouble ahead," he yelled at the soldiers. "Get your weapons ready!" He circled back to Rae and Alan. "You two, down to the end of the caravan! Stay behind the soldiers! And watch your backs! Desert bandits are sneaky devils, got to have eyes in the back of your head. Watch out."

One of the guides, riding up to keep the pack camels in line, tore past. Alan's Arabic was good enough for him to shout, "Who's coming?"

"Desert people!" The guide turned to fling one more word over his shoulder.

"Bad!"

◇ CHAPTER TWELVE ◇

The cloud of dust on the horizon became a line of camels streaking straight toward them. There were about a dozen, with one rider out in front leading the troop. The camels' hooves pounded across the waves of sand. As they came closer, the sight became blinding, with the bright sun flashing on the scimitars they waved aloft. The shrill howls coming from their throats sent a cascade of chills down Alan's spine.

Alan saw Saul lean toward Jason and tell him something. Then Jason wheeled his camel around and headed back. "Rae! Alan! Get going, you two, Saul wants you behind the soldiers! No fooling around!" He was off in

a swirl of sand to rejoin Isaac and Saul up front.

Fooling around? Why did Jason always have to sound so superior? As if I were ten years old, Alan thought. He yanked the scimitar from his belt and made a swipe at the air before glancing at Rae.

She was doing the same. Imagine, a girl ready to fight like a man. In the world of his father's castle, such an idea would have been unthinkable.

They headed their camels back toward the soldiers, who were unslinging their bows. If only he were on horseback, Alan thought, instead of perched in midair on this swaying monster! "How can you fight sitting on a camel?"

"Why not? You can fight on a horse." Rae's eyes were fever-bright with excitement. "What's the big difference?"

Mahmud rode up with the other guides to join the soldiers. "Who are they?" Rae called out. A torrent of Arabic poured from Mahmud too fast for Alan to understand.

"What was that all about?"

"He says they're a group of outcast Bedouins who prey on travelers. But there's one good thing. They probably don't know we have armed soldiers with us. Maybe they'll get scared and run away when they see them."

But the Bedouins kept coming across the sands. Saul spurred his camel back again to yell at the soldiers, "Don't attack till I give the signal!" Then he galloped to where Isaac and Jason waited.

Soon the attackers were close enough for Alan to see their faces. The leader's features were fixed in a frightening grimace under his headdress. The captain and Jason urged their camels forward to confront them. But Saul waved them back. "Stay back—I'll go first!"

So the action would start any minute now. Alan felt a sinking feeling in his stomach. His first real fight. He'd be up against an enemy who'd actually be trying to kill him. Could he remember everything Jason had taught him?

He sliced the air again with his scimitar. With the back of his palm he wiped the sweat from his forehead. Squinting, he kept his eyes fixed on Saul, a lone figure riding forward to meet the Bedouins. Was there still a chance the attackers would melt away once they caught sight of the soldiers?

"A-i-i-ee!" With a frightful scream the Bedouin leader, scimitar waving on high, dashed his camel straight at Saul. From Jason's lessons, Alan reviewed the way to meet such an attack. Engage the other's scimitar with a parry and lunge upward for the heart.

To his amazement, Saul simply sheathed his weapon. As the Bedouin came up to him and swung, Saul ducked under the curved blade and leaped from his camel straight at the attacker. Both crashed to the ground, Saul on top. The bandit's weapon flew from his grasp and fell useless on the sand. The other Bedouins reined their camels in sharply and stared.

What they saw was Saul gripping the djellaba, the loose

robe, of their stunned and disarmed leader. A moment
later Saul had hauled the Bedouin to his feet by the hair
and was holding the sharp blade of his scimitar against
his foe's neck. Wide-eyed, Alan urged his camel nearer.
He heard Saul speak a few words of Arabic to the leader.
The Bedouin waved his arm at his men. They backed their
camels away.

Saul yelled to Isaac. "Show him the medal, Captain."

Isaac dismounted from his camel and strode over to
where Saul held the Bedouin motionless. He took the
medallion out and held it before the man's eyes.

"Do you recognize this symbol?" Isaac pulled the
man's face closer to the medal. The leader moved his
head in a nod as far as Saul's grip would allow him.
"Good. Now listen to me, you miserable excuse for a son
of Abraham! Doesn't this order from His Majesty allow
us to pass without interference?" After a brief pause, the
head moved up and down in agreement.

"Behold, our captain is merciful!" Saul released his
hold. He picked up the leader's scimitar and headdress
and held them out. "You may take your pack of thieves
back to your tents. Before His Majesty's soldiers make
you sorry you ever started this!"

Mumbling apologies, the Bedouin remounted his camel
and led his men back over the sand ridge where they had
first appeared. They were soon lost from sight. The
soldiers and guides gave a cheer and put up their weapons.
Alan followed Rae, who spurred her camel up to where

Saul stood. When her camel knelt, she jumped off and embraced him. "Father, you were wonderful!"

Alan dismounted and came forward to shake Saul's hand. "Well done, sir! But what was that you said to them—that these soldiers were the caliph's own?"

Saul grinned at him. "A little exaggeration never hurts. That's your lesson for today, Alan. Whenever possible, do the unexpected." His eyebrows lifted. "And pray like anything!"

Walking back to his camel, Alan felt the same mixture of relief and disappointment he'd experienced after the pirate ship incident. Am I always going to be a spectator, he asked himself, sitting and watching the action? Can't I ever do anything to make Rae look at me the way she looked at Saul just now?

"Mount up!" Mahmud's hand waved the caravan forward.

The days that followed grew hotter. Captain Isaac had them change into Arab clothing, the flowing loose djellaba and the kaffiyeh, the light headcloth. Right away Alan felt his body released from bondage, free and cool. Why didn't they wear such sensible garments during the hot summers in Toulon?

And the Arab headdress completely covered Rae's hair. In the flowing robe, she might now be taken for an Arab youth. He inspected her and felt reassured. Much safer, in this dangerous wasteland.

Farther south, the Tigris widened. Whenever they

camped near the river, Alan stripped to his underclothes and jumped in for a quick swim. One thing his father had insisted upon was that he not be afraid of the water. So he had learned to swim in the Mediterranean as a child.

Of the other four, only the captain joined Alan, parting the water with a slow but determined breaststroke. The others used the river only to bathe, Saul standing guard when it was Rae's turn.

Alan invited Rae to swim with him, but she refused. He was puzzled. "Don't you know how?"

"I never learned!" She tossed her head and strode away. He stared after her in disbelief. Had he finally found something he could do that she couldn't? And Jason didn't know how, either. Sailors who couldn't swim!

Late one scorching afternoon, Rae stood on the shore watching Alan swim. She was frowning and biting her lip. Suddenly she unfastened her robe and tossed it aside. In her linen shift, she waded into the river up to her neck. With an abrupt lunge, she launched herself forward, kicking and flailing her arms. But instead of moving forward, she sank. A moment later, she came up sputtering.

With quick strokes, Alan swam to her side. "Here, let me show you how." He grasped her hands and pulled her forward. "Stretch out and kick. You'll stay afloat, honest. You're not going to sink!"

Rae kicked hard, and they began to move through the water. "Great!" she panted.

Alan laughed. "See? It's easy!" It felt wonderful to

be Rae's teacher. He pulled her through the cool water, smiling into her wet, glowing face.

He pulled her to her feet. "Now you're ready for the next step."

"Already?" She frowned and tugged her shift down. It clung to her.

Alan tried not to stare. "Here, stretch out across my arms. When I start moving, kick the way you just did. At the same time, keep your fingers together and move your arms like this." He demonstrated, pushing the water back one arm at a time. "Don't be afraid, I won't let go of you!"

Rae thrashed away as Alan moved her along. She was actually in his arms. Or on them, anyway. She was a sea creature he had just captured. It was a moment he wanted to last forever.

A roar from the riverbank startled him into dropping her. She sank and bobbed up, blowing water and looking mad.

"Rachel! You come right out of there!" It was Saul. "What's going on?" He held up her robe. "Come and put this on right now! And you, boy, turn your back and swim off!"

Rae slammed the water with both hands. "What's wrong with learning how to swim! And cooling off a little?"

"Never mind! Do as I say!"

"Sorry, Rae." Alan turned and swam away quickly.

Saul didn't mention the swimming lesson afterward. But his voice was sharper than usual when he spoke to Alan. And there were no more swimming lessons.

Despite the heat, the lessons in Arabic continued. Whether it was side by side on their camels, or waiting for the guides to prepare supper at the campsites, it made no difference. Rae hammered away at him like a soldier attacking the enemy. Still, her resolve produced results. Little by little, he became more fluent.

The days became weeks. The rippled expanse of sand offered no guideposts. The river seemed to flow on and on endlessly. The sun baked everything beneath it. Everyone became irritable. Alan began to despair of ever reaching their destination.

One morning, after breaking camp and moving on for several hours, the caravan came to one of the ever-present hills of sand. When Mahmud reached the top, he halted his camel and motioned for the captain and the others to come forward. What was happening? More trouble? The five of them spurred ahead of the guards and lined up alongside the guide.

Mahmud pointed to the southern horizon. Outlined against it and shimmering like a mirage in the blazing sunlight Alan could see a great curving wall. Above it glinted the shining tops of towers. Mahmud grinned and waved his hand toward the sight.

"Observe the minarets, Sheik Isaac! Baghdad!"

◇ CHAPTER THIRTEEN ◇

Alan was surprised. "A big wall inside the city? What's that for?" The caravan had just passed through the gates of Baghdad. The wall he was staring at was curved and massive.

Rae swung her head about. "That's the wall around Harun-al-Rashid's palace. He's the caliph. Look over there, you can just see the tip of the palace dome."

The captain, riding by, overheard. "Wait till we visit the palace tomorrow. There are even more walls inside!"

Alan urged his camel on to catch up with the captain.

"Does that wall go all around the palace?"

"Completely. Baghdad was the dream of Harun's grandfather, the famous Al Mansur. He chose this spot on the Tigris for his capital city. He had his architects lay out a great circle in the sand to form the circumference of his city-to-be. When it was finished, cloths soaked in naphtha were packed around it and set afire. So Baghdad began as a city of flames."

Mahmud led the caravan through a noisy marketplace. On a side street they stopped at a sprawling building with a large courtyard.

"Read what that says, Alan." Ever the teacher, Rae pointed to a sign over the entrance.

Alan leaned forward on his camel. His last few lessons had been on Arabic script. "Home—no, House! House of—the—uh—something—Traveler—"

Rae sighed. "Well, you're pretty close. House of the Welcome Traveler."

"We'll be staying here till we finish our business," Captain Isaac said as they all dismounted. "Dinner first, then a good night's sleep. Meanwhile we'll hope for an invitation from the caliph." He turned to Mahmud. "Please go to the palace directly and inform His Majesty that I've arrived. Say I'll be pleased to see him at his convenience." Mahmud saluted and left.

Emerging to meet his new guests, the roly-poly innkeeper first frowned to see that they were foreigners, but was mollified when they addressed him in Arabic. He

called for grooms to take charge of the camels. Stowing away belongings didn't take Alan long. It was still early in the day, and he was anxious to see the sights. When he came back out to the courtyard, Rae was already there, pacing about.

"What took you so long, slowpoke! I'm dying to explore that marketplace. Let's go see what it's like—"

Jason, coming inside, overheard Rae and frowned. "Wait a minute, you two can't just skip off by yourselves. Rae, you'd better ask your father about sightseeing." She nodded and ran back into the inn to return a moment later with Saul.

Rae's father was obviously not happy about having his daughter wander about Baghdad with Alan. "Well—all right. As long as Jason goes with you. But don't go far, remember. And don't be gone long."

Jason nodded. "If you're sure you don't need me here—"

"Positive. I wouldn't have any peace of mind if you weren't with these two." Saul turned to his daughter. "Now make sure your kaffiyeh hides your hair. You're supposed to be a boy, remember? And don't speak to anyone, not a soul. No one is supposed to know you're a girl, understand?" He tugged at an ear, frowning.

"Yes, Father, I won't forget, I promise."

"And you," Saul's eyes bored into Alan's. "Make sure she keeps her mouth shut. That goes for you, too. Remember, you're both foreigners here. This is a different

world. And do what Jason says. If she gets into any kind of trouble, I'll hold you responsible, too!"

Why is he talking to me as if I'm a nitwit, Alan thought. He's making Jason our caretaker. We can't even go without him. And yet he's handing me the responsibility. But he's her father, I can't argue with him. "I'll do my best, sir."

Saul grunted without smiling and went quickly back into the inn.

Alan looked at Jason. "You were here once before, right? Well, then—" He pointed to the bustling square. "Where should we go first?"

Jason shrugged. "All of Baghdad's worth seeing. Makes no difference." He thought for a moment. "I know what, let's head for the waterfront. You've never seen anything like it—ships from all over the world."

"I was just a child when I was here, I hardly remember a thing," Rae said.

As they entered the square, Alan's mouth opened in astonishment. "Look! Aren't those—" A page in the bestiary of Father Paulus fluttered in his mind. "Elephants?"

A line of huge beasts with wrinkled gray skin and long trunks dangling almost to the ground lumbered by.

Rae pointed. "Look what's on their backs." Each elephant was draped with brocade woven in peacock-feather designs and glittering with gold and silver threads. The beasts stayed in single file, each using its trunk to

grasp the tail of the one in front. And each was controlled by a man holding on to a curved stick hooked behind the elephant's ear.

"Where are they going?" Alan wondered.

Jason waved his hand. "Over to the palace, probably. These elephants belong to the caliph. I hear they use them in battle."

Alan shook his head. "I'd hate to have one of them step on me!" They watched the elephant parade until it turned the corner and was gone.

Again they stopped to stare when they reached the Tigris waterfront.

"Just look at all those ships!" Rae pointed. As far as the eye could see, ships of all kinds rode on the water. Some were plainly rigged for war. Others, much smaller, were obviously for pleasure.

"See those, with the strings of flags?" Jason pointed out a fleet of very small boats with prows and sterns that curved upward and outward. "They're called zouraks. They use them to get from one part of Baghdad to another."

They walked along. Rae kept stopping. "Look, over there. Can you imagine the different cargoes that came in one of these ships? Perfumes and fruits from Persia, spices from India, slaves from Ethiopia! See, there's one from Cathay—probably brought fine silks!"

They studied the oddly shaped great ship, high at the bow and stern and low in the center. A dragon's head

formed the prow, the face blue melting into green, with red fire spurting from the mouth. "That's the most fantastic of all," Alan said.

Jason led them back from the harbor through a maze of twisting streets. With Rae walking between them, Alan remembered Saul's warning that he was responsible for Rae. He'd better not lose her in these crowds. Alan saw groups of men and boys walking with their arms across each other's shoulders. Should he put his arm around Rae? Wasn't that what Saul would want, to make sure they wouldn't become parted in the crowd? But a sudden wash of shyness stopped him from reaching out. Besides, Jason was there. Alan's hand stayed at his side.

Jason suddenly halted and scratched his beard. "Wait, I'm not sure this is the right way."

Alan glanced at the sun. "I think it's that way. We were heading west before."

"It's through here!" Rae darted ahead of them into one of the narrow streets. A crowd of people blocked her off. They could see her white kaffiyeh flashing in and out of the myriad other kaffiyehs and turbans.

Suddenly Alan and Jason found themselves completely hemmed in by a throng milling about some stalls in a crowded bazaar. Bargaining was going on at a high pitch. Hawkers were shrilly proclaiming their wares, pulling at the passersby, wheedling, "Come, feel how fine this fabric is!" Colorful rugs, silky scarves, clothing and sandals, and foods of every kind were for sale. The scent of cinnamon

and the aroma of meat being grilled over braziers filled the air.

Alan grasped Jason's arm. "Where's Rae? I don't see her!"

"You were supposed to watch!" Jason glared at Alan. "Well, don't just stand there, come on! We've got to find her!" Hot with anger at Jason's tone, Alan followed him, pushing his way through the crowd.

"Look, Jason!" Far down the street at the end of the bazaar, Alan spotted a flash of red among the kaffiyehs and turbans. "There she is! That's her hair, I can tell! She's lost her headdress."

He and Jason set off at a run, shoving aside everyone in their way. Behind them a trail of fists waved aloft amid shrieked curses. "Over there!" Alan yelled. He was horrified to see that Rae was being dragged along by two men. "Those men—they've got her!" One of them had pinioned her arms behind her back. The other's hand was over her mouth. "Let's go!"

They drew their scimitars. "Out of the way!" shouted Jason. At the sight of their weapons, the crush of people parted before them. A moment later they were right behind the two Arabs who were pulling the struggling Rae along. Alan and Jason dashed around and barred their way.

When they saw the drawn scimitars pointing in their direction, the two abductors halted. Rae's eyes widened when she spied her comrades. Alan could hear the muffled voice coming from behind the hand that covered her mouth.

"Let the girl go!" yelled Jason in Arabic.

"What business is it of yours?" The large one pinning Rae's hands scowled. "She's an infidel spy. Fair game for the slave market!"

The shorter man leered. "With that hair, she'll fetch a good price!" He spat through crooked, gapped teeth. "What are you after, a share of what we get?"

Alan fished for the right words. "She belongs to us!"

"Oho, hear that accent?" cried the first. He raised his voice. "Listen, people, these men are infidel spies! They're threatening to kill us! Help! Help us!"

As a muttering began in the crowd, a ring quickly formed around the group. Alan could see a flash of knives being drawn.

He nudged Jason. "What do we do now?"

"Easy does it. Keep your scimitar pointing right at their throats."

Rae took advantage of her captors' distraction. She raised one foot and stomped hard on the instep of the man holding her arms. "Ai-ee!" he howled in pain, and let go. With her elbow she jabbed sharply into the other's stomach. An "Oof!" exploded from his mouth, and he doubled over. His hand fell from her face. Alan grabbed Rae and pulled her over between Jason and himself.

"You all right?" asked Jason, keeping his eyes on the kidnappers.

"Yes, but I'm angry!" Rae reached into her robe and drew her scimitar. "They didn't know I had this. Let's run them through!" She waved her scimitar under the noses of the two Arabs, who cowered back.

A voice shouted from the crowd. "The little infidel may be a girl, but she shows a man's spirit!"

"Maybe she's from the land of warrior-women!" yelled another.

Someone laughed. Then another. Soon, the whole crowd was roaring with laughter. Jason and Alan looked about them with astonishment. The mob that a moment ago had been so menacing was now enjoying the joke. Even Rae was surprised.

A sudden commotion erupted at the rear of the ring surrounding them. Everyone's head turned.

"Make way! Make way!" A squad of armed soldiers was forcing the crowd to part. Through the passageway came an ornate palanquin of black ebony and silver, carried on the shoulders of eight bearers. Ruby-colored velvet drapes enclosed the windows. From inside, a ringing voice called out the order, "Stop!" The palanquin was set down. The crowd fell silent.

One of the soldiers opened the palanquin door and stood stiffly at attention. A man of regal bearing in a glittering silken robe and a white turban stepped out into the circle. Dark-eyed and slim of figure, he moved toward the center with deliberate steps. At once the entire crowd fell to their knees, heads bowed low to the ground. Only

the three shipmates were still on their feet.

Jason turned to Rae and Alan, who were standing wide-eyed. Jason let out a low whistle.

"Who is that?" whispered Rae.

"The caliph of Baghdad himself!"

◇ CHAPTER FOURTEEN ◇

The caliph's voice rang out. "What's going on here?"

The only sounds came from the bazaar just beyond. No one spoke or even moved. The caliph strode over and prodded the closest of the prostrate men with his foot. "You, rise! Speak!"

A thin little man with a pockmarked face scrambled to his feet. "O Most Reverend among the Faithful, those infidels were threatening those two. With their scimitars!" He pointed to the kidnappers, who had their noses pressed to the ground.

"And why were the infidels doing that?"

"Those two were dragging that infidel woman away." He waved a hand toward Rae. "She's a spy, see?"

The caliph walked slowly over and prodded one of Rae's captors. "Stand up!" Visibly trembling, the burly fellow rose to his feet. "How do you know she's a spy?"

"Her kaffiyeh fell off, O Most Esteemed Majesty, and we saw she was no boy! Our women don't go running around the streets dressed as men. So she must be an infidel spy!"

"A reasonable conclusion." The caliph turned to the thin little man. "Tell me, what happened when the infidels," he said as he pointed at Jason and Alan, "threatened our citizens?"

"The girl—pardon—the infidel spy freed herself by stomping on that one's foot and punching this one's stomach." A titter went through the prostrate group.

The caliph tried to suppress a smile. "And then?"

"Then everyone started laughing to see two big fellows getting punched by a slip of a girl—even if she is an infidel."

"Enough!" Now the caliph turned his full attention to the three infidels.

"Show respect." Jason followed his own muttered advice by sheathing his scimitar and bowing low. Alan and Rae did the same.

"Your Majesty." Jason's Arabic was practiced. "We're members of the crew of the ship *Devora*. We wear these garments because we've been traveling through the desert for many days."

"You speak our language well for an infidel. What's

your name?"

"I'm Jason, Your Majesty. This gentleman is Alan, count of Toulon in the Frankish kingdom. And the young lady is Rachel, daughter of our bos'n. We're part of Captain Isaac's crew on the Radanite ship *Devora*."

"Isaac? Isaac the Radanite?" A broad smile brightened the caliph's face. "You mean the captain who brought me presents from Charlemagne? And carried my gift of a white elephant back to him? That Isaac?"

"The very same, Your Majesty."

"Listen, that man is lying!" burst out Rachel, pointing at her kidnapper. "He knocked my kaffiyeh off on purpose. He and his evil friend were going to sell me in the slave market!"

"Rae, shh!" Jason hissed. "Don't speak till you're spoken to!"

Harun-al-Rashid chuckled. "Never mind. While we cannot quite approve of her actions, we must admit that the young lady is brave. And also speaks our language well." He turned and called over one of his soldiers. Pointing to the men who had seized Rae, he commanded, "Take these two away. We'll deal with them later!"

The kidnappers threw themselves at the caliph's feet. "Mercy, O Kindest of All Rulers! Mercy in the name of Allah! We were only doing our duty—"

"Silence! You've shamed us before these most welcome visitors!"

He made a motion and the soldiers led the two away.

Harun turned to Rae. "And what is a charming young lady doing aboard a Radanite ship?"

"My father, Saul, is the bos'n of the *Devora*. When my mother died, he began taking me on his voyages. I'm the cabin boy."

"And a very competent sailor she is, Your Majesty," said Alan.

"And you?" The caliph eyed Alan. "A Frankish nobleman working as a seaman?"

Alan tried to choose his words carefully. "Your Majesty, I went seeking adventure—"

"Reason enough. When I was younger, seeking adventure was a most important quest. Jason, can you tell me when your captain is planning to visit the palace?"

"Our guide is already at the palace, Your Majesty. Even now he awaits your invitation."

"Good. We'll make all the arrangements." Harun suddenly became aware that a number of his subjects were still prostrate. He clapped his hands. "You may all rise now and carry on. Go with Allah!" Slowly, they got to their feet and bowed. "One moment. Does anyone know where this young lady's kaffiyeh happens to be?"

People looked around, shaking their heads. Then one man came forward, looking abashed. He held Rae's white headdress out. "It was in the street, Your Majesty." Rae snatched it from his hand and covered her hair.

"That's better." The caliph waved his hand in a motion of dismissal and the crowd dispersed. He turned to

Jason. "Where are you staying?"

"At the House of the Welcome Traveler, Your Majesty."

"Ah, yes, I know where that is. Quite a distance from here. Permit me to offer you the use of my humble palanquin. It can carry four people very comfortably." He waved a hand and a soldier opened the palanquin door.

The arrival of the royal palanquin before the House of the Welcome Traveler caused quite a stir. Inside the vehicle, Alan lifted a corner of the velvet curtain and saw people pouring out of the inn to watch the spectacle. Alighting after Rae and Jason, he was dismayed to see Saul and the captain in the forefront of the crowd. Saul had put Rae in *his* charge, as well as Jason's. How was he going to explain what happened?

While Alan was debating how to begin, a grim-faced Saul strode up to the three. "Where in thunder have you been? I said a *short* stroll, not a day's journey!" Frowning, he took hold of Rae's robe. "How did this get torn?"

"We can explain, Saul—" began Jason.

A sudden murmur arose from the crowd. All except the five foreigners fell to their knees and bowed their heads to the ground. First one royally shod foot appeared through the palanquin door, followed by a second. Harun-al-Rashid stepped forward and faced Saul.

"We do not understand your Frankish tongue, good sir." Harun's tone was commanding. "But if you speak our language, we can ease your mind as to what happened. This young lady was mistaken for a spy. Your young

people deserve only praise for saving her with their brave actions."

It was the first time Alan had ever seen Saul at a loss for words. The bos'n stammered his thanks and shifted from one foot to another.

The captain stepped forward and bowed deeply. "Your Majesty, I sent word the moment we arrived."

"Captain Isaac!" Alan was surprised to see how warmly the caliph grasped Isaac's hand. "We remember your last visit fondly. Tell me, did you manage to get the baby elephant safely to your King Charles?"

"Indeed we did, Your Majesty. Even though getting the beast over the Alps and to the palace was a bit of a trial. But the king was delighted with all your gifts, truly delighted."

"Good. We're happy to be at peace with your people at last." Harun stopped and glanced down at the people still prostrate. He clapped his hands. "You may all rise. Go with Allah."

He turned back to Isaac. "Now, how about tomorrow, can we plan your visit to the palace? With your companions, of course."

"It will be our pleasure, Your Majesty." Isaac bowed again.

"Good, it's settled. Let us say before evening, just after the late afternoon prayer. May Allah watch over you!" He bowed and reentered the palanquin, which was raised and carried swiftly away.

The awed innkeeper ushered his infidel guests back into the inn. With smiles and low bows, he declared that their slightest wish was his to obey.

Alan nudged Rae. "Certainly pays to be in the caliph's good graces."

She grinned. "He sure kept us out of trouble."

Once inside, Saul became his angry self. "Listen, Alan, I told you it was your job to watch out."

Rae cut off his tirade. "It was all my fault, Father! We were trying to find our way back, but it wasn't easy. So I ran ahead and those nasty men noticed me. They knocked off my kaffiyeh and grabbed me."

Alan tried a different tack. "Don't be mad at Rae, sir. You would've been proud of what she did. We didn't even have to fight! She put both of them out of commission herself!" He went through a pantomime of Rae's actions.

"You did that?" Saul fought hard to keep a frowning face, but lost out to a wide grin. He picked up Rae and swung her in the air. "You did all that by yourself?"

"If I'd had the chance to draw my scimitar," said Rae when he put her down, "I'd have run them both through, one-two!"

Saul turned to Alan, the grin gone from his face. "As for you, young man, you should never have let this happen! You know Rachel well enough to realize how fast she moves. Why weren't you more careful? I made you responsible—"

Alan opened his mouth and closed it, no words came

out. How could he explain to her father that having Jason
along had changed everything?

"Just a minute, Saul." Jason came forward. "I'm more
to blame than Alan. I got us all lost. We were just trying
to figure out which way to go."

The captain clapped his hands. "That's enough, Jason!
All right, Saul, stop blaming everyone. Perhaps I should
have forbidden anyone to go sightseeing. Anyway, all's
well that ends well. Let's enjoy our supper."

And they did. It was a sumptuous meal of lamb roasted
with apricots and lemons, rice with saffron, and couscous.
For dessert, there were fresh figs and pomegranates. The
innkeeper served his guests himself and fussed over them
endlessly.

Alan was glad to be seated on a cushion next to Rae,
who was exclaiming over the delicacies. Did she appreciate his not complaining to Saul about her reckless-
ness? She was the one who had really caused the
trouble. And, miracle of miracles, Jason had come
to his defense. But their misadventure had led to meeting the caliph himself. Who would have imagined that
could happen right in a crowded bazaar! And what a
friend the caliph was. Look how he had defended them
against Saul's anger.

Lying in bed that night, he tried to imagine what the
palace would be like. Would there be golden lions and
singing birds as there were in Constantinople? As if ex-
ploring the exotic city weren't adventure enough, Rae

would be there, too.

She had disliked him for such a long time. From the first day, when she mocked him for being a stowaway, for living off of others' hard work. She laughed because he was such a clumsy dolt at seamanship. And she looked down on him for being illiterate. Imagine, he was the only one on the *Devora* unable to read or write. There were plenty of reasons to reject him, to keep him at a distance.

But once she had hugged him. He could still feel the surprise of her cheek against his. And the press of her wet body against his arms in the river.

At dinner, she paid a lot more attention to him than to Jason. Jason sat there with a long face, watching them out of the corner of his eye. And Alan was the one she had wanted to go sightseeing with. So had she finally changed her opinion of him?

Alan tossed and turned for a long while, mulling the question over. How could it happen that the more she taunted him, the more he cared about her? Is that what love is?

But would she ever feel about him the way he felt about her?

He wondered: does her heart flip-flop like mine when we're close?

◇ CHAPTER FIFTEEN ◇

he call to prayer was echoing from the minarets when Alan awoke. He lay still for a moment, watching the first rays of the sun sketching patterns on the walls. He was aware of a faint aroma that made him feel hungry. Of course, it was coffee. He'd had his first taste of that fragrant drink during the trek through the mountains.

Jason was still asleep, so Alan dressed quickly and went in search of breakfast. In the dining room he was served the thick, delicious mixture in a tiny porcelain cup, along with small twisted pieces of a sweet pastry covered with powdered sugar. Sugar! Mmm, nothing like it in Toulon, where honey was the only sweetener.

Captain Isaac strode into the room and sat across from

him. "Morning, Alan! Jason told me after dinner last night that he was glad to have you along yesterday. It's no joke, to be surrounded by a mob in a strange country."

Alan swallowed his pastry and licked the sugar from his fingers. "But Rae really freed herself, sir. You should've seen her!"

"Quite a young woman, isn't she? She told me how you three confronted them." He sipped his coffee. "You're certainly not the same frightened boy we hauled up from the hold back in Marseilles. When I agreed to take you on as crew, I've got to admit I had my doubts. But there's no question, you've grown up."

"Thank you, sir." Alan rubbed the bristles of an early beard that had begun on his chin. He was proud of it. "Still, I wonder if I'm tough enough to take on Hugo. That's what's waiting for me in Toulon."

"Hugo?" The captain frowned. "I wouldn't worry about him yet. Plenty of time to figure out ways to deal with him. A great Jewish scholar once said, 'He who has an envious eye and hates his fellow-creatures will be led to destruction.'"

"Sounds like he knew my cousin Hugo."

Isaac looked up. "Ah, here come the others. Good morning, Saul, Jason, Rachel. Breakfast is delicious. After you finish, we'll gather the gifts for the caliph."

"Isn't it exciting!" Rachel twirled around, so that her new cream-colored robe fluttered about her. "The palace—I didn't even get there last time we were here. I can

hardly wait!"

"You were only a child then." Saul rubbed his chin with his knuckles as he watched her.

Jason grinned. "And now you're a regular Amazon."

"Oh, you." Rae gave him a dig in the ribs with her elbow.

Watching them, Alan felt a stab of jealousy. Maybe his suspicion was right—there was something between Rae and Jason. He'd been worrying about it ever since Jason had warned him not to act like a typical nobleman. As if noblemen were all alike, any more than sailors!

Anyway, he told himself, now we're in Baghdad. No desert heat and bandits to deal with. If only Saul keeps Jason busy, I'll have a chance to be with Rae, without a million shipboard duties and a whole crew gaping. A chance for us to get to know each other better.

But what about her father? Will he object? And will I always be competing with Jason? But we're in Baghdad; they call it the city of magic. Who knows, anything's possible here!

After the muezzin had chanted his evening call to prayer, the *Devora* crew gathered in front of the inn with boxes bearing gifts stacked up before them.

"How are we getting to the palace?" asked Alan. "Horses or camels?"

"Neither. I've ordered palanquins." The captain pointed down the street. "And here they come."

There were five small palanquins to carry them, and a

sixth for the gifts. Oh, the luxury of it, to be borne aloft like a king and carried off to a palace. On this journey, Alan reflected, I've been on a horse's back, then on a camel's back, and now on men's backs. Stowing away on the *Devora* certainly changed my life.

He kept watching from the palanquin window for a sight of the palace. Finally, part of the great curved wall came into view. The parade of palanquins was halted by the guards at the gate and waved through. The first wall was unbelievably thick, and the tunnel through it seemed endless. Next came a second wall, then a moat, and finally a third wall, so high that Alan had to crane his neck to see the top. Harun's grandfather, who built this palace, must have been worried about enemies.

At last the palanquins stopped and they all stepped out, gazing about. Before them rose a huge arched doorway whose elaborately carved bronze doors stood open. As they passed under the arch, Alan noticed a great black cloth draped on the wall over the doorway.

He nudged Rae. "Never saw a flag like that before—black."

"The family flag," she told him, "the flag of the Abbasid caliphs."

The brilliance of the throne room dazzled his eyes. He had never seen so many flaming torches and sconces with lighted candles. Another surprise was the circle of armed soldiers that reached from one side of the entrance to the other. A courtier ushered their group to the royal

presence.

Alan could see no musicians, but strains of music, plaintive as a wail, floated to his ears. His feet sank into the luxury of thick wool rugs woven in intricate patterns. The air was filled with the sweet scent of incense. It reminded Alan of the garden his mother tended in summer.

On a billowy divan heaped with pillows, Harun-al-Rashid reclined. He wore a lustrous silk robe woven entirely of gold threads and a matching turban. Next to him sat the most elaborately dressed woman Alan had ever seen. Robed in a gown of rich brocade, she flashed dark eyes above a white silk veil that covered the lower half of her face. Her feet were shod in slippers studded with gleaming jewels, and about her neck hung ropes of luminous pearls.

In front of the royal divan, Captain Isaac sank to his knees. Before the others could do the same, Harun rose and lifted the captain to his feet.

"No, no, my old friend. Your place is here." He motioned for the captain to join him on the divan. Then he clapped his hands. Servants darted over with huge pillows, which they placed on the rug near the divan for the other four.

Harun turned. "This is my dear wife, Zubayda. My dear, these are the boldest sailors of all, the Radanites. Remember, I told you about them. They're People of the Book. They think nothing of traveling from one end of the world to the other!"

The captain bowed. "Your Majesties," he said, "I bring you greetings from King Charlemagne. He wishes to renew the pledge of friendship made during our last mission."

"Excellent." A smile wreathed the caliph's face. "Please assure him that we have the same desire."

"And if it pleases Your Majesty, we have brought a few small gifts as tokens of our friendship." Saul helped Isaac unwrap the bundles. As the gifts emerged, Isaac described each one.

"A pair of swords fashioned by the best blacksmith in the kingdom. Two shields of leather and iron. For Her Majesty, a jeweled headdress. Six mantles of combed wool. For His Majesty, a belt woven of gold, from the land of the Vikings. And from that land, also, intricate carvings of ivory. Rare beaver skins from Khazaria. A bell cast in bronze and silver. And finally, a supply of pure lead for your alchemists."

The caliph rubbed his hands in delight. "These offerings are most pleasing to us! I shall be hard put to find any half as fine for your Charlemagne." He watched with approval as the gifts were borne away. "Now we shall have a little refreshment and entertainment." He clapped his hands.

Servants brought silver trays heaped with food: skewers holding pieces of roast lamb and fowl, exotic fruits, and sweetmeats. Others came with cups and pitchers of sweet fruit juices. Meanwhile, Alan noticed the source of the

music, a group of musicians sitting in a far corner. Some were plucking away at strings and others blew into what looked like long hollow pieces of wood. A drummer began tapping out a rhythm. Alan found the music haunting, completely different from anything he had ever heard.

As the music swelled, from one of the doorways emerged a chain of dancing girls in filmy, floating costumes. Their glowing eyes were rimmed with kohl. The dancers swirled and swayed about the guests in time to the music. Alan had never seen such a spectacle, and he glanced at Jason and Saul. Like himself, they were so bewitched by the sight, they were hardly eating. Even Rae appeared spellbound.

"Justice! In the name of Allah, I demand justice! He who does wrong must be punished!" The shouts came from the arched doorway opposite the caliph. One of the palace guards rushed toward the caliph, waving a scimitar wildly, yelling the angry words over and over.

Every head turned. Could this sudden interruption be part of the entertainment? The torchlight glinted on the man's weapon. As the interloper crashed through their line, the dancing girls screamed and fled, cowering. The spectators shrank back, frightened. So the guard was no actor. Shrieking, with a contorted face, he had the look of a madman. And he was heading straight for Harun-al-Rashid.

For an awful moment, everyone in the room seemed frozen in place. The music had ceased as suddenly as the

dance. There was no sound except the angry shouts for vengeance. The soldiers stationed around the outer walls stared at their fellow soldier in confusion. As the wild guardsman thrust himself past Alan toward Harun, Alan sucked in his breath.

Without thinking, Alan dove for his legs. Still yelling, the guardsman fell heavily to the ground. Alan pinned him down, but the guard twisted free and pointed his scimitar at Alan's throat. In desperation, Alan swung his fist in a circle. It struck sharply against the man's hand and the weapon spun away from his grasp. With new-found strength, Alan jammed his other fist into the guard's belly, making him gasp. Alan rolled over on top of him and sat on his chest, holding both arms pinned to the floor.

By this time, the guards had surrounded them. As they held their scimitars at the would-be assassin's throat, Alan, still breathing hard, stood up.

Harun, visibly pale, was on his feet. "Bring that man here!" The guards dragged the man forward. "Who are you? How dare you speak of taking the life of your caliph?"

The man stared defiantly at Harun. "I am Farouk. I have always served you faithfully! But last month you condemned my son to death. For a crime he never committed! Your people seized him. They wouldn't listen. He's in prison, they're going to kill him. And he's innocent! In the name of Allah, show him mercy!" He began

to weep bitterly.

"Why did you not come to us for redress?" The anger faded from Harun's voice. "We will consider this matter later." He waved a hand. "Take him away." He turned to Alan. "Come here, young man."

When Alan stood before him, the caliph put his hand on his shoulder. "Your quick action merits great praise. You saved us from certain death."

"Anyone would have done the same." How smart Rae had been, to keep hammering in those lessons in Arabic. Without them, he wouldn't have known what was going on.

"It was a brave act and must not go unrewarded." The caliph crossed his arms and looked about the throne room. His eyes returned to Alan. "What reward can suffice? Gratitude is not enough. Ask what you will. Gold, precious jewels, anything! Your wish shall be granted."

Alan was dumbfounded. He turned to Rae. "Did I hear him right? That I can ask for anything I want—anything at all?"

She nodded. "Anything—even a fortune."

What should he ask for? He stared at Rae. Her green eyes were wide but she said nothing more. Alan looked at the others. The captain's lips formed a half smile, Saul raised his eyebrows and shrugged, Jason eyed him curiously, or maybe enviously. None offered a single suggestion. The decision had to be his alone.

Gold? Gems?

A sudden inspiration made him turn back to the caliph.

"Your Majesty, a traveler who once came to our castle in Toulon told us about your wonderful teller of stories. A woman named Scher—Schera—" Alan searched his memory.

Harun's eyes lit up. "You mean the Princess Scheherazade's name has reached the land of the Franks? Oh, yes, she is here."

"The only reward I ask is to hear one of her stories!"

"That is all?"

"I may never have another such chance, Your Majesty."

"You are an unusual young man." He called to an attendant nearby. "Musa, see that the princess is asked to appear." Harun seated himself back on the divan and motioned the others to resume their places. He bent toward Alan. "Alan of Toulon, where did you learn to speak our language? Not many Franks even attempt it."

Alan pointed. "Rachel here was my teacher, Your Majesty. But I still have a lot to learn."

"A woman of many qualities. I like that. Both a teacher and a maiden-warrior!"

It was the first time Alan had seen Rae blush.

A young woman dressed in rustling silks approached the divan, sank to her knees, and bowed. "You summoned me, Your Highness?"

"Yes, I have a delightful assignment for you. This young man, who comes from a distant land, has just saved us

from an assassin's sword. I offered him gold and jewels, but the only reward he desires is one of your stories."

Princess Scheherazade rose, her dark eyes glowed. Alan saw she was younger than the caliph's wife. Slender, her face partly veiled, she appeared beautiful and mysterious.

She sank onto a pillow next to where Alan sat. "Is there any special story you wish to hear, O handsome youth?"

Alan could feel his face flame. "Whatever you like, Princess."

She nodded, thought for a moment, and began. Her voice was clear and musical. The room grew quiet. Everyone leaned forward to listen.

"First, my friends, close your eyes. Now, take a deep breath. Again. And once more, breathe deeply. Let your thoughts drift free. Your senses are taking in the fragrance of the incense. And remembering the glow of the tapers. Now, open your eyes. Your spirits are refreshed, your minds are cleansed, you are ready to venture to far-away lands.

"Picture a forest, dark and leafy with foliage. Birds of a dazzling blue are darting and singing overhead.

"Suddenly, a brilliant green frog jumps out of a splashing stream. In a flash, it hops into the hand of a young peasant girl sitting on the bank...."

◇ CHAPTER SIXTEEN ◇

And they look at each other with glee, and dance about in a ring. For they know that the evil spirits are vanquished and there will be peace in the land from that time forth. And they live together ever after in joy and gladness under Allah's blue skies." There was a hush as the Princess finished the tale, followed by a burst of applause from the listeners.

Rae was the first to speak. "That's the most wonderful story I ever heard." She spoke dreamily.

So she had fallen under the enchantment, too. "Thank you, Princess," Alan said to Scheherazade. "I'll remember this evening for the rest of my life."

Harun clapped his hands in delight. "There will be

more to remember, my young champion. We invite you all to be our guests for as long as you desire. There's plenty of room in the palace!"

The Radanites looked at each other.

"Very kind of Your Majesty to make such a generous offer," said the captain. "But we're here on a mission for a Frankish nobleman. Just a short stay, just enough time to transact our affairs."

"Nonsense, business can wait! You've come so far! We insist that you stay!" Harun reached his hand out to Alan. "Come, sit here next to your captain."

Flushing, Alan rose and bowed. "Thank you, Your Majesty." He could feel Rae's eyes on him as he moved to the divan.

"The words of the Prophet promise a great reward for those who do good deeds." The caliph lifted his hands above his head and recited, "As for him whose scales are heavy with such deeds, he shall enter into Paradise!" He turned to Isaac. "And it is our wish that this palace be a paradise for your young champion."

The captain held out both hands, palms up. "Who can resist such an invitation? Thank you, Your Majesty, we accept. But we must be back in the Mediterranean by December." He stroked his beard. "Although staying here until the hottest days in the desert are past is probably a good idea."

"Then it's settled. We shall send for your things at the inn. Musa, will you see that rooms are readied for our

five guests?"

Musa bowed, then looked at the caliph quizzically. "Your Highness, what about the girl? The harem, perhaps?"

Saul jumped to his feet. "The harem? Not my daughter!"

Alan was startled. Did being in the harem mean being treated as one of the caliph's women?

"Oh, noble guest, please do not be alarmed." The caliph's wife, Zubayda, entered the conversation. "She will be our guest. She will have her own room, apart from the women in the harem. No one will harm her."

The caliph laughed. "I assure you, you need have no worries about your daughter. Do you Westerners think that any woman who enters a man's harem becomes the property of that man? The palace harem is only the women's section, and Rachel is welcome to stay there."

"Oh, Father, please let me go!" Rae was on her feet, too. "I've always wondered what a harem was like."

"Now you shall have your wish." Zubayda patted the divan. "Come, sit by me, and I'll tell you what to expect."

Harun-al-Rashid was true to his word. During the weeks that followed, Alan felt he was living in a dream world. And he was not alone. Rae, too, was caught up in the splendor of palace life.

On their first morning at the palace, Alan saw Rae in women's clothes for the first time. All alone, sipping coffee, for a moment he did not recognize the slim figure that

slipped into the dining room from the harem entrance. Rae was wearing an elaborate vest of gold and silver embroidery over a long white robe. Her eyes were accented with thin lines of black, and her lips were reddened with rouge. As she came up to him, Alan was aware of the scent of a delicate perfume. They were alone.

"Rae? Is it really you?" He drew in his breath. "You look so different."

She whirled about. "What do you think?"

And only months ago he'd thought she was a cabin boy. A boy! All of a sudden he was talking to a stranger. He had to choose his words with care. "You're—beautiful!"

It was apparently the right thing to say. Rae laughed. "I'm glad you think so." She came a little closer. "Alan—?"

The air about him felt thin, like on a mountaintop, so that it was hard to breathe. "What?"

"I just wanted to tell you. When the caliph said you could have anything you wanted, I expected you to ask for gold or jewels. I'll bet it's what most men would've chosen. But to ask for a story—to appreciate that more than riches!" Her eyes were green silk. They stared at him. "Whatever made you think of that?"

He moistened his lips. "The offer was tempting. But on the ship the crew acted as if I were a useless nobleman's son. Jason never lets me forget that I'm no sailor. So how could they stand me if I came back with a fortune?"

Rae frowned. "Does what they think matter so much

to you?"

"It's what *you* think that matters."

She was silent for a moment. "But you hardly ever spoke to me, as if you thought you were better than me."

He looked amazed. "Me?"

"Yes, you! Anyway, how did you know about Scheherazade?"

"That traveler back home said he'd been all over the world, but her storytelling was what he remembered best. So I thought, when would I ever again have a chance to hear such a wonder?"

Rae's scarlet lips curved in a smile. "Alan, you're full of surprises!"

"Am I?" He smiled back. "Well, so are you. Maybe we just got off to a bad start."

She made a face. "Was I such a tough teacher?"

"Never mind." He was trying not to let her nearness melt his brains. "Here we are in this magical place. Let's make the most of it."

A giggle escaped her. "On one condition—"

He gave a mock sigh. "What is it?"

Her smile was demure. "As long as you speak only in Arabic." She moved even closer. Her perfume was making him dizzy. Her lips were parted, her skin had a slight flush. He moved to hold her in his arms.

"What's going on?" Saul had appeared, along with the captain and Jason. Rachel sprang aside and faced him. He peered at her. "Rachel, what've you done to yourself?"

She pirouetted. "What do you think, Father? Alan thinks it's beautiful."

Saul glared at Alan and turned back to Rae. "Well, I think it's terrible! What are you trying to be, one of the caliph's dancing girls?"

Rae's face turned into a storm cloud. "But that's how women dress around here—what harm is there in it, anyway?"

Her father sighed. "Rachel, you have fresh young skin, you don't need all that paint covering it up! Go back and scrub it all off your face. Right now! Go!"

Rae flounced off. Her father looked at the others and shrugged. Alan said nothing, but for once he wondered if Saul was right. True, his first impression of the new Rae had stirred his blood, but perhaps it was the soft, feminine clothing. The makeup made her look much older. The face etched in his mind was that of the glowing sea creature, standing in the Tigris. Her delicate features and tousled hair needed no improvements.

Captain Isaac shook his head. "Your daughter's not a little girl anymore, Saul. She's a woman now."

Saul glowered at Alan. "And you encouraged her!"

"What can you expect from a nobleman?" said Jason, with a shrug.

An angry retort came to Alan's lips, but died there. What was the point of quibbling with Jason? Face paint or no face paint, Rae looked beautiful to him. But it was a lot more than her appearance that he loved. It was her

spirit, nothing ever daunted her for long.

Oh, he'd known all along about her courage. But her taunts had hurt him. Except now he realized that her snubs must have been a kind of barrier, a way of putting him off until she knew him better. Her words didn't come from a deep-seated ill will toward Alan. They were a young girl's shell of protection.

As the days passed, Alan was secretly glad that Captain Isaac and his two Radanite companions had to spend most of their time outside the palace, trading their wares for bolts of silk fabrics and boxes filled with spices. It meant that Alan and Rae were free to be together. Not alone, but at least together.

Endless entertainment awaited them. They were taken on sightseeing trips, where they marveled at the exquisite architecture and art of the mosques. The caliph arranged for his best swordsman to give them both practice in scimitar fighting. And for two glorious weeks they were guests aboard the huge Royal Barge as it was rowed down the Tigris all the way to the Persian Gulf and back to Baghdad. During that time, they were always in the presence of some of the caliph's people. Though he ached to do otherwise, Alan made a point of behaving very formally toward Rae. He didn't want a single whisper to get back to her father.

After the barge trip, Alan was especially excited about meeting the Royal Astronomer. Ibn Nasr was delighted to find that Alan knew the constellations. "Most

Westerners I have met are ignorant of these things," he
said, running his fingers through his white hair, which
sprouted in all directions.

Rae stood by, quiet and wide-eyed, while Ibn Nasr
showed them how to use an instrument called an astrolabe
to measure the positions of the stars. Then he drew pic-
tures to demonstrate his method of plotting the orbits of
the planets around the earth. "These techniques were
worked out by the Greek astronomers of long ago. Here,
look." He pulled out a fat book from his large library and
opened it to the title page. "Claudius Ptolemy's *Al
Magister,* the greatest work on astronomy we have. Written over six hundred years ago!"

The following evening at dinner, Rae nibbled at a date
and turned to Alan. "Did you understand everything Ibn
Nasr was saying?"

"Mmm, sort of."

"You're lucky to know about stars and constellations."
She sighed. "Wish I did."

He finished chewing an apricot. "Look, why don't we
go outside after dinner? The sky's clear. It should be a
perfect night for observing." Imagine, Rae was asking *him*
to teach *her* something! He could hardly wait for the
meal to end. The two of them slipped out together
when everyone rose to go into the throne room for the
entertainment.

In the garden, where they stood alone, the air was soft
and fragrant with the scent of blossoms. Above them,

the sky was a canopy of sparkling jewels. It was quiet, except for faint strains of music floating from the palace.

"See there, in the west, that very bright star?"

Rae nodded and moved closer to his outstretched arm.

"That's Sirius. Remember the time Samuel fell asleep at the steering oar?"

"Who could ever forget that night?"

"That was the star that told me what was happening. And there, right above our heads—" She moved closer. A new scent filled his nostrils, a perfume more pungent than the aroma of the flowers. He felt light-headed and had to search for what he had been about to say. "Uh— there's Cygnus the Swan. See, it's like a cross."

"Mmm." She lowered her head and looked at him, she was smiling. "The way you figured out how the ship was moving off course, and not the star—it was wonderful!" Her hand slowly crept up and cupped his cheek with her palm, her touch delicate but firm. A burst of music came from inside. His own hand reached up and covered hers. His outstretched arm somehow wound itself about her shoulders. The stars were inside his head now, reeling.

Suddenly she pulled away. "Alan, wait!"

"What's the matter?"

"Maybe we shouldn't be doing this."

"What? But Rae, I love you!" He was surprised at his own words. "Don't you feel the same way about me?"

"Oh, I—I—" She seemed ready to burst into tears.

"I know. It's Jason, isn't it? You're in love with him—"

Her interruption was quick and fierce. "No, no, it's not that at all! Jason and I—well, we grew up together. Our families were close friends. Before my mother died, she told me that there was an agreement about us. They made it when we were very young." Her voice died.

Alan looked away from her up into the sky. A swift falling star burned its way across the northern horizon. A bad omen. "I understand, Rae. Foolish of me not to see it sooner. No wonder Jason's been needling me, telling me to keep away from you." His brain suddenly caught up with part of her answer. "Then it's just a family thing? And you don't love him?"

"I didn't say that. I do care about Jason. I care about him a lot. But I keep thinking of him as my brother. It's a different kind of love, I suppose...."

He turned to face her. "And what do you feel about me?"

"About you?" She came very close and looked into his eyes. "I don't know. But I've never felt this way about anyone before. Does that mean I'm in love?"

"Oh, Rae." His hands were on her shoulders, ready to draw her close.

Her voice whispered something. Was it in Hebrew?

His cheek came closer to hers. "What did you say?"

"From the Song of Solomon. 'Arise, my love, my fair one, and come away....Let me see thy countenance, let me hear thy voice.'"

Her words streaked through his brain like the falling

star. *She loves me! Not Jason, but me! She said it!*

He could bear it no longer and pulled her to him.

"Rachel!" Saul's voice sounded loud and harsh in the quiet. The two of them sprang apart and wheeled around to face him. "Go indoors this instant!"

"But, Father—"

"Do as I say!"

Rae gave Alan a frantic glance and ran from the garden. Was that a strangled sob he heard?

Red-beard stood there, arms akimbo. Alan was a stowaway again on the deck of the *Devora,* waiting to be thrown to the fishes.

"Listen to me, Alan! I forbid any intimacy between you and my daughter!" Saul raised his hand to intercept Alan's attempt to speak. "Oh, I can see that this place is bound to affect young people. All that music and dancing. But Rachel is still too young for any such thoughts."

"But I wasn't—I would never—"

"She's not for you, boy! You come from a different world. Keep that in mind. And remember, you are a guest of the Radanites. Don't take advantage of the situation!"

"Advantage? Look, sir, I have the highest regard for Rachel. I'd give my life for her!" He stopped and expelled a breath. "Is it because I'm not of your people? That's what you really hold against me, isn't it?"

Saul's jaw tightened. "There's nothing for us to discuss. And see to it that there never is!" He turned on his heel

and stalked back to the palace.

Alan stood motionless for a minute. What crime had he committed? Angrily, he began stomping back and forth. Once, he stopped and shook his fist at the Swan, as if what happened was the fault of the stars. Being so close to Rae in the garden had been the most perfect moment of his life. And Saul's words had destroyed everything.

Oh, he knew why Saul was furious. He was angry because he found them in each other's arms. But would he have carried on like that if it were Jason? With Alan, it was a different story altogether. Because no matter what Alan did, he'd still be a Christian and not a Radanite. Even if he could beat Jason with the scimitar. Even if he became wiser than Captain Isaac. To them he'd always be an outsider.

And Rachel would always be as far beyond his reach as the stars.

⟡ CHAPTER SEVENTEEN ⟡

Alan wondered how Rae's father would treat him after the confrontation in the garden. He needn't have worried. Red-beard was remote, but polite. But Rae never even mentioned what had happened. Was she, too, desperately trying to make the most of the time that was left? When her father and Jason were away with the captain, she stayed as close to Alan as possible. So, at least while they were in Baghdad, they could enjoy being together.

Except there were few chances for them to be really alone. One afternoon, on one of the day trips on the Royal Barge, Alan could stand it no longer. Refreshments were being served, and the other members of the party

were sipping cool drinks and nibbling sweetmeats as they lolled in the shade of a striped canopy. Everyone was chatting and enjoying the freshness of the air.

Alan turned to Rae and spoke in Frankish. "Rae, ever since that night in the garden, we haven't really talked to each other. You know what I mean. Whatever we do, there's always someone around. And time's passing—"

She put down her drink and stared at him. "You mean like right now? But isn't it rude of us not to be speaking in Arabic? Rude to our hosts?"

"No, it's not!" he exclaimed. He didn't want to call attention to them, so he lowered his voice. "Why shouldn't we use our own language once in a while? It's a lot easier for me, I'll tell you that. Besides, you're changing the subject. What about us?"

"Oh, Alan." Rae bit her lip. "It's all I think about, no matter what we're doing. First thing in the morning, and the last thing at night. Oh, being in Baghdad's exciting, there's no place like this. Living like royalty! But you and I—that's altogether different. Sometimes I can hardly breathe."

"You, too?" Little jolts of delight ran through every vein in his body. "Then you do care about me, you do!"

Her eyebrows went up. "Care? Do fish swim? Of course I care, that's the whole trouble."

"But that's not trouble, it's—wonderful! It's like being on top of the highest mountain in the whole world! Just you and I up there, no one can even come near us."

She sighed. "You make it sound so simple, Alan. If only it could be like that."

"You mean, because your father objects?"

She nodded. "You know how it is with him. I've tried to talk to him, to explain, to make him see how I feel—he refuses to listen!"

"But it's me you care about, not Jason," he said fiercely. "How can you even think about Jason now!"

Her gray-green eyes clouded. "Oh, Alan, things are a lot more complicated than that. It's not Jason, not really. Do you expect me to run away and never see my father again? Don't ask me to choose between you and him."

"So is it better if you and I part and never see each other again?" The minute he said the words, he regretted them, such a look of misery crossed her face. "Look, we'll find a way, somehow."

She smiled in the old cheeky way. "I think I've been in love with you since the first day—I just couldn't admit it."

"What? You acted like you hated me." But he was smiling, too. If he could only kiss her; she was so close. He had to be content with covering her soft, cool hand with his. Rae cared, nothing else really mattered. She had loved him all along!

So for the final two weeks in Baghdad, Alan was happy. Every night he fell asleep asking himself question after question. Should he talk to the captain about becoming a Radanite? What would he have to do? Would it be hard

to give up being a Christian? And what about his obligations to his mother? And there were the lands and the castle. It was his job to defend them: he owed it to his father. So how could he spend his life at sea?

It was impossible to make any long-term plans until he had taken care of Hugo.

He hated to see the carefree days pass. So many problems loomed in the future. But finally their last night in the caliph's palace came. It was to be especially splendid. Harun-al-Rashid had ordered a great feast to be prepared. The musicians played and the dancers dipped and whirled for hours on end. And Scheherazade came to finish the evening with a memorable story.

Before everyone dispersed to sleep, the caliph asked Alan to approach. To everyone's surprise, he embraced him.

"Your brave deed will go down in the annals of my reign. The name of Alan of Toulon shall never be forgotten by Islam!"

All the people in the throne room applauded. Harun released Alan and called to one of the courtiers.

"Since you would take no gold or jewels as a reward, I want you to have this token of my thanks. It will grant you free passage anywhere in Islam." He hung a gold medallion around Alan's neck. When Alan looked down, he was stunned. Engraved on it were the same Arabic words as those on the medallion that Captain Isaac wore: Harun, Commander of the Faithful. He now wore the

very medallion that had gotten them out of trouble twice during the journey to Baghdad!

Alan stammered his thanks. The rest of that evening became a blur in his memory—Jason congratulating him, and even Saul. Captain Isaac bidding the caliph farewell. Rae smiling at him the same way she had when he had asked for a story as a reward.

Soon enough, he found himself high on the back of a camel, but no longer riding alongside Rae. She now rode beside her father. The caravan was following the same trail along the Tigris and across the desert sands as before. Only this time, instead of six soldiers to keep them safe, Harun had sent a whole squadron of cavalry to accompany them.

After supper on the first night they camped, Rae motioned for Alan to follow her over to where her camel knelt in the sand. She undid her pack and took out a small leather box.

"Look, Alan." She opened the lid.

He saw a group of little porcelain pots and some brushes. "What are those?"

"A present from the women in the harem. The beauty paints they put on me that time in the palace." She put her finger up to her lips. "But don't breathe a word to my father."

He frowned. "What do you want those for? You don't need them—you're perfect without them!"

"What?" She stared at him. "You said I looked

beautiful that day!"

"But...." He shifted from one foot to another. "That wasn't really the paints, it was the clothes, your hair, everything. You were dressed like a girl for the first time! So, naturally...." He floundered.

"What did I look like before, an idiot?" she snapped. "You're worse than my father! To think that I thought you were different!" A bright spot of red stood out in each of her cheeks.

"But don't you see, in the West it's not the same!" Why couldn't he make her understand? "In Toulon, no nice girl would ever—"

"So now I'm not even a nice girl!" Her glare scorched him. "Is that how you judge people? You're just a pompous nobleman, that's what you are! You could never be a Radanite, no matter how many medals you won!" She snapped the case shut, stuck it back in her pack, and hurried back to the campfire.

Speechless and miserable, he stumbled after her. Why had he ever argued about the silly paints, anyway? Now Saul had gotten his wish. To Rae he had become just a landlubber again. A foreigner from another world.

After that night, the days and weeks filed past Alan in mechanical precision. The Tigris drifted off somewhere, camels changed into horses, and the desert changed into mountains. Everything that had seemed so new and exciting on the way from Trebizond to Baghdad became meaningless routine on the way back. Even the food had

lost its savor and no longer seemed exotic.

When he did try to draw Rae aside to talk, she would regard him coolly and give the briefest answer possible. Yet at times he could hear her chattering away to the other three. If Jason or Isaac noticed the tension between him and Rae, they gave no sign.

It seemed impossible that his remarks about the beauty paints had stirred such anger in her. Was her father continually reminding her of the pledge with Jason? She had declared her love that afternoon on the Royal Barge. Was she sorry afterward? Maybe she wasn't sure of herself. Maybe Saul's words kept nagging at her inwardly.

She was so independent and feisty—that's what he loved about her! Still, perhaps she wasn't ready yet to flout Saul's wishes, to become serious about an outsider. So Alan's dislike of the face paints might have been only the spark that set off the real turmoil inside her. Perhaps things weren't as bad as they seemed.

He had to turn the clock back somehow. He had to get back the Rae who had offered her love so openly on the Royal Barge.

Trebizond, at last. Welcoming shouts of "Shalom!" rang out on both sides. The *Devora* lay where they had left her, moored snugly. The crew was full of anxious questions.

"What took you so long? You said you'd only stay a short time."

"How did the caliph—"

Captain Isaac motioned for silence. "Plenty of time for stories tonight! First, let's get all this cargo stored below. Then, make the *Devora* shipshape. We're off to Constantinople at sunrise!"

The crew cheered and fell to work, unloading the packs of silks and spices and the boxes of gifts for Charlemagne. The captain and Saul left to buy supplies as well as a new set of slaves to man the oars. The Saxons had been sold off the day they arrived in Trebizond.

Alan was happy to lose himself in real physical work as a sailor again. His muscles were now equal to the task of lifting heavy bales without staggering under their weight. Out of the corner of his eye, he watched Rae hurrying about, checking to see if things were in place. His heart gave a little wrench at the sight of her old blue cap from under which a few locks of red always escaped.

After supper that evening, the captain told how Rae had narrowly escaped being sold on the slave market. When the crew heard how Alan had foiled an assassin bent on killing Harun-al-Rashid, they shouted their approval. At this point, Alan peeked over to where Rae was sitting across from him. To his delight, her mouth was curved in a little smile.

"Who'd've thought that puny stowaway we hauled on deck would have the guts to do all that," Samuel

marveled.

"Wait, there's more." The captain told them how Alan had refused offers of gold and jewels and had asked only for a story from Scheherazade.

The crew members whistled. "Tell us, Alan," said Nathan, the oldest of them, with a sly glance, "what was this storyteller like? Did she cuddle up to you before she started? Was that part of the deal?"

"Wait a minute!" Alan said. "You don't understand. She—she was—"

Rae interrupted. "Don't ask him! What do men know about what women are like! She wasn't just pretty, she could cast a spell. The minute she began speaking, her voice and her words sent you into a faraway land."

"So where did you wind up with this beauty, Alan? In Cathay?" interrupted Nathan. Everyone laughed. But the laughter sounded good-natured to Alan, and he laughed with them.

"Alan, show them what the caliph gave you," ordered Jason. At the sight of the medallion similar to Captain Isaac's, the crew members eyed one another in surprise. The group gathered around Alan, slapping him on the back.

"By God," said a grinning Moises, "our stowaway's become a man!"

For the moment, he forgot all about Saul's bitter words that night in the desert. He was one of them, he was a Radanite! And Rae had smiled.

At sunrise, the mooring ropes were cast off and the drumbeat began. Slowly the rowers moved the *Devora* away from the wharf and out into the Black Sea. At the helm, Samuel pushed the steering oar to head the ship in a westerly direction. Once out of the harbor, Saul sent Alan and Nathan aloft to untie the sail. Fortunately, the morning breeze came from the east. Once the sail had snapped taut, the drum ceased and the rowers shipped their oars.

On the third night out, Alan's turn for the late watch came up. The first-quarter moon had already set, and the night sky was diamond-studded with stars. The air held the crispness of early autumn. Down below, the steady beat of the rowing drum told him that the wind had lessened.

He made his way to the bow and stretched out on deck for his favorite pastime of finding the constellations. Overhead blinked the star Deneb in the Northern Cross. To the north, he made out the crooked tail of Draco the Dragon, which ended just midway between the Big and Little Bears. Alan thought about his visit with the caliph's royal astronomer. Could he ever learn as much about the heavens as that man? Perhaps Father Paulus knew someone skilled in astronomy at the abbey.

A light touch on his arm made him jump and sit up. The rose-petal scent told him it was Rae. "What—?"

Touching a finger to her lips, she scrunched down beside him. Her voice was a whisper. "Alan, I couldn't

sleep. I don't know what got into me back there in the desert. Maybe it was that scene with my father in the garden. After that nothing was really the same."

"No, it was all my fault! What right did I have to give you orders?" The curve of her cheek in the dimness filled him with bliss.

She shook her head. "Oh, it wasn't that, really, it was everything...."

His fingertips brushed her hair. "Everything? What do you mean?"

A sigh escaped her. "Leaving the palace, saying all those good-byes, knowing we might never see them again." She fiddled with a curl just above her ear. "Wondering what would happen to us."

"What about you and Jason? That's what your father wants, right?"

"Let's not talk about that now. I can't help wondering if I'll ever again be as happy as we were back there...or if the whole thing will just be something to dream over when I'm an old woman."

He couldn't help laughing. "You an old woman? You could never be old!"

"Mmm. Now who's the dreamer? I'm going to be sixteen before long."

He took her hand in his; hers felt warm. "Now who's being silly? We've got years and years ahead of us—maybe we'll get back to Baghdad someday. But it doesn't matter; we'll find a way to be together. It'll be marvelous!"

She leaned forward, and her lips found his. Hers were smooth and delicate. His arms went around her, and they clung together.

All too soon she pulled away. "We're wrecking ship's discipline," she whispered. "Next watch'll be coming out." With a little smile, she disappeared into the shadows.

He couldn't believe his good fortune. It was all going to come out the way he wanted, in spite of Red-beard, and in spite of Jason. The ache in the pit of his stomach was gone, and the stars winked back the message, *Rae loves me!*

◇ CHAPTER EIGHTEEN ◇

On the morning that the *Devora* entered the Bosporus Strait, Captain Isaac announced that they would be stopping at Constantinople only briefly. "Just to fill the water casks. And I have a personal errand." Wails of disappointment rose from the crew. Like Alan, they still dreamed of the chance to see Empress Irene's palace.

When the captain returned and the rowers had taken the *Devora* out into the Sea of Marmara, he called Alan, Jason, Saul, and Rae into his cabin. "Listen, we're going to stop over in Rome."

"Rome?" Saul frowned. "We never stop there on our way home!"

Jason tugged at an ear. "Why Rome, Captain? I want

to get home to my folks!"

Captain Isaac put his hand up. "Of course, we all want to get back home to Marseilles. But wait'll you hear what's going to happen."

"What's that, sir?" Alan had never been in Rome.

"If the rumor I heard in Constantinople is true, Pope Leo will crown King Charlemagne as Holy Roman Emperor!"

Jason whistled in surprise.

"And that's supposed to happen soon?" asked Saul.

"Christmas Day. My good Byzantine friends told me the pope is doing this to foil Empress Irene's ambitions. Otherwise, she might force the pope to make *her* the first Holy Roman Empress."

Rae clapped her hands together. "What a show that'll be!"

Saul turned to Isaac. "But can we make it? It's almost November."

"With God's will and a steady wind, we'll do it!"

On the twenty-fourth of December, the rowers nosed the *Devora* next to a pier in Ostia, the seaport of Rome. Captain Isaac appointed Nathan and Samuel in charge of the Radanite ship. Five horses were rented for the twenty-mile ride to Rome. Rae made a point of not riding next to Alan, but her glance told him that it wasn't her idea.

For late December, the weather was mild, with no sign of snow on the ground. Hazy spirals rose from chimneys and made the air smoky.

Alan had heard tales of Rome, but the splendor of the city staggered him. He marveled at the great walls and gates, and the triumphal arches stretching over wide avenues. Captain Isaac acted as guide, pointing out how much of the glamour of the ancient days of Imperial Rome had been restored since the destruction of the city four hundred years earlier.

Throngs celebrating the Christmas holidays crowded the streets. The air resounded with the clanging of church bells. Visiting country people, priests, and merchants were being jostled by armed soldiers. Vendors were busy hawking their wares, from food to religious relics. The doorways of churches were jammed with pilgrims coming and going. Holiday excitement was in the air and rumors abounded. Every face bore a sense of expectancy.

"Wait'll you see the Colosseum," the captain said to Rae and Alan. "The arena where the gladiators fought. And where wild beasts were set upon the Christians. Did you know that? There's a saying there: 'So long as the Colosseum stands, Rome will stand. When the Colosseum falls, Rome will fall, and with her the world.'"

"Let's hope the Romans keep it in good repair," said Rae.

"I don't think we have to worry," added Alan, "as long as Charlemagne is in charge."

Isaac led them to an inn where they could stay the night. After they had supped, Alan tried to get a chance to speak to Rae alone. But Saul kept her at his side until bedtime.

The next morning, they followed the crowd outside the walls of Rome to the Vatican hill. A long colonnade ran straight upward to the porch of St. Peter's Basilica. "Isn't this exciting?" Rae had managed to edge next to Alan. "Just think, poems and stories will be written about this day!"

"Come this way." Captain Isaac led them all around the perimeter of the crowd. "I have a friend—" A soldier dressed in the armor of the Vatican Guard motioned for them to approach and led them through the crowd to a spot near the steps. Alan took advantage of the crowd to stay close to Rae.

"Look—the royal party! Aren't we lucky to get this close!" Alan had never seen his King Charles in person. Charlemagne glittered in a tunic of gold cloth that was partly covered by a military cloak. On his feet, jeweled boots flashed in the pale sunlight of the Roman morning.

Above, on the Vatican porch, stood Pope Leo the Third robed in white. Behind him were his shaven clergy, resplendent in their vestments, men with tense faces and watchful eyes. Charlemagne ascended the stairs to receive the ceremonial kiss of welcome. The chatter of the crowd ceased. Alan smiled to see his tall king stoop to accommodate the smaller man. Then, the procession passed slowly through the porch into the church. The choir

followed, chanting a hymn of praise. Behind them came a large group of Frankish nobles.

Alan said, in a low tone, "If my father were alive, he would've been among that group."

Rae's smile was impish. "You're the count of Toulon, why don't you join them?"

Alan shook his head. "Right now I'm a Radanite!"

The crowd began pushing into the great nave of St. Peter's, and from there into the transept, the part that crossed the nave. The captain's soldier friend led them through a side door to a place nearer the altar. The walls of the transept were covered with rich mosaics and sacred paintings.

The soldier pointed to a brilliant cross of light that shone above them. "There's over a thousand candles in that cross!"

Hundreds of candles also illuminated the altar, over which hung a tapestried canopy. Charlemagne moved to the altar and dropped to his knees. A hush fell over the crowd. Alan could hear the distant, thin wail of a baby somewhere at the back of the church. Pope Leo moved toward Charlemagne, a golden circlet gleaming in his hands. As Charlemagne rose, the pope placed the crown upon the monarch's head.

"Long life to Charles Augustus, crowned by God, the great and peacemaking emperor of the Romans!"

The pope's cry was repeated three times by the crowd. A loud chorus of rejoicing broke from the choir. The

music swelled to the rafters. Now the pope and Charlemagne changed postures. The pope knelt to the first western Holy Roman Emperor in history.

Tall and erect, his bronzed face impassive, Charlemagne towered over the pope. To Alan, he looked like a stalwart tree. What was his king thinking of? Was this the greatest triumph of his life? Or was it lonely to be placed on such a dazzling pinnacle? Would he have to fear for his life and always be surrounded by soldiers, as was Harun-al-Rashid?

The pope went through the ritual of the Mass. As soon as the service was finished, the captain motioned for the crew to follow him out a side door. "Saul will take you back to the inn. Start for Ostia as soon as you can. I'll meet you at the *Devora*."

With her typical boldness, Rae asked, "Where are you going, Captain Isaac?"

"Rachel!" Saul chastised his daughter.

"A brief errand, Rachel. Nothing to concern yourself about."

When the four returned to Ostia, the Radanite crew demanded to hear every detail of the coronation. Still glowing with excitement, Rae acted out what had happened. Broad-shouldered, handsome Charlemagne stooping to receive a kiss on each cheek from short, thin Pope Leo. Charlemagne kneeling to have the golden crown placed on his head. The hosannas of the choir. The Frankish nobles scrambling to keep up with Charlemagne

as he strode from St. Peter's.

Not until late afternoon did the captain return, accompanied by six armed men. The soldiers dismounted and left their horses in charge of one of them. The other five followed Captain Isaac up the gangplank. Alan and the others stared in wonder. When they recognized the leader, the crew all fell to their knees.

"No need," said Charlemagne. "Please rise." His clear voice rang out.

"Our guests," announced the captain, "will sail with us to Marseilles." He clapped his hands. "Prepare to cast off. Nathan, get the rowers ready." To Charlemagne, he said, "If you'll follow me, sir, I'll show you and your men to your quarters."

As the *Devora* eased out of her berth, no two Radanites passed each other without asking the same question. "Charlemagne himself aboard! What could it mean?" In the ship's galley, little Moises raised his eyes to heaven. "I can't believe it! I'm going to be cooking for the emperor himself!"

The next morning, after breakfast, Saul motioned to Alan. "Captain wants to see you up forward."

"Me?"

"Yes, and don't be too long. There's some rope to be spliced."

At the bow, Captain Isaac was deep in conversation with Charlemagne. Alan waited nearby until they finished. He could hear the rush of water as the *Devora*'s bow split

the Mediterranean and the crack of the sail as the wind gusted.

"Come here, young man." Charlemagne motioned to him. Alan approached and began to kneel before his emperor. "Not necessary, Alan of Toulon. Captain Isaac has told me of the plot against you in Toulon." He put his massive hand on Alan's shoulder. "I knew your father, Gerard, well. He was a good fighter and a loyal knight. It was a sad day when I heard of his death."

"Thank you, Your Majesty."

"We've been discussing how to handle your problem. Your villainous cousin and his two-faced bishop will have a little surprise arranged for them."

Charlemagne himself coming to his aid! Alan raised his chin. "Begging Your Majesty's pardon, but I had it in mind to handle the problem myself. There's no need to waste your valuable time."

Charlemagne laughed. "Well spoken, lad! Just what your father would have said! But you forget one thing." His face turned grim, the deep lines about his mouth stood out. "Isaac tells me that you heard them plotting to raise an army against me. Is that true?"

"I'm afraid so, Your Majesty. With Simon of Brittany—"

"That traitor!" Charlemagne roared. "He'll wish he'd never been born!" He banged his fist on the ship's rail. "Well, that means I have as large a stake in this as you do."

"Don't forget me," put in the captain dryly. "That bishop has plans for me, too."

"So, you see, Alan, we're all in this together." Charlemagne said. "But there's one difference between you and me."

"What's that, Your Majesty?" Alan asked.

Charlemagne winked. "I happen to have more resources handy!"

atching a brisk winter breeze, the *Devora* slipped through the narrow passage between the islands of Corsica and Sardinia and headed for the coast of Provence. At twilight on the last day of December, the rowers brought her into the harbor of Marseilles and sculled her gently to her wharf.

From the day Charlemagne came aboard, Rae had been flinging questions at Alan. "What's going on with the emperor aboard? Why is he going back to Marseilles with us? Why isn't he staying in Rome for the celebration?"

Alan kept trying to put her off. He wanted to spare her any involvement in his situation. But it was no use. Finally, he broke down and told her why he had fled from

the castle. "I just didn't know what to do. Then I realized that the one place I could get away was on the *Devora.*"

"What a horrible person! And he's your cousin!" Rae had her hand on the hilt of her scimitar, and Alan knew what her next move would be.

He covered her hand with his. "I'll bet you'd like to meet him and run him through!"

"That's what he deserves!"

"Don't worry, it's not your problem. And look at the help I'm getting—from Charlemagne himself!" In a way, he would have liked to face Hugo alone.

Rae's voice sharpened. "Why didn't you tell me all this when you first came aboard? You only said someone was after you."

Alan shrugged. "Maybe it was better not to go crying for sympathy. To have everyone yelling at me. I sure had a lot to learn."

Rae fingered the medallion hanging against his chest. "And now you're a hero." Her voice grew coaxing. "Aren't you going to tell me what Charlemagne and the captain are planning?"

He shook his head. "How can I? They haven't told me a thing."

The toss of her head told him she didn't quite believe him. But it was the truth. Neither the emperor nor the captain had given him a hint of what they were planning. And now that they had reached Marseilles, it was frustrating to be in the dark. Didn't they trust him? Were

they going to leave him completely out of the picture?

His last night on the *Devora* seemed endless. Just being back in his homeland, glimpsing the wharves of Marseilles, thinking that his mother and the castle were only a few hours away, had his stomach turning. And he would come face to face with his cousin Hugo at last. He had waited so long for this moment. Now that it was almost at hand, he didn't know how he'd get through the last hours till the confrontation. Sleep was impossible; he tossed for hours. Was he really good enough to outfox Hugo in a duel?

In the morning, as soon as the gangplank was down, the soldiers left the ship and returned a short time later with horses. Charlemagne thanked the assembled crew for a fine voyage, shook the captain's hand, nodded briefly to Alan, wished all a happy new year, and strode down the gangplank to the waiting horse. On horseback, the brawny warrior appeared even more formidable. Watching him lead his troop away, Alan could understand why the mere sight of him could make enemy armies tremble.

"Jason!" Captain Isaac's order brought the sailor forward. "Get a horse at the livery stable and ride to the castle of Toulon. Inform Master Hugo that the *Devora* has arrived safely in port. And the Baghdad mission has been completed successfully. Tell him I'll be bringing the goods to the castle this afternoon. Mind you, not a word about Alan's being on this ship!"

"Yes, Captain. Understood."

"Good. Wait for us at the castle gate."

Captain Isaac then turned his attention to renting a large cart and horse. The many bolts of silk and the boxes of pepper, cardamom, cinnamon, coriander, and other spices were hauled up from the hold and loaded on the cart. When all the goods meant for Hugo were stacked, a large canvas tarpaulin was spread over the load and tied down.

"Alan, come here." The captain pointed to the cart. "Just before we leave, I want you to hop into the back of the cart and slide under the tarpaulin. There's plenty of space for you. Mind, it's important for you to stay hidden till I come and give you the word."

"Hidden?" Would he have no part in defeating Hugo? "But—"

The captain waved his hand. "I know how you feel about Hugo. But this is the emperor's plan. Trust us, Alan."

"But, Captain—" They were treating him like that puny stowaway. "I just—all I really want is a chance to settle with Hugo myself!"

"Don't worry, your moment will come." Captain Isaac looked up toward the sun. "We'll be leaving soon. Saul will ride with me. Perhaps you'd like to say good-bye to the others."

Alan nodded. Did he mean Rae? He went up the gangplank and over toward the bow, where she was leaning on the rail, watching. "I guess this is good-bye, Rae. For now, anyway...." Sleepless last night, he'd tried to

figure out his farewell words. Maybe it would be better for Rae to forget him. Hugo was a formidable fighter.

She stared at him. He came closer and looked into the sea-green of her eyes. "Rae, you're some teacher."

"Now you're going to be a nobleman instead of a sailor. I guess we'll never see each other again."

"What?" He didn't care who was watching, he took her hand. "Don't say that! Toulon isn't far from Marseilles."

Her smile changed to a grin. "Practically next door. You can come and visit when I'm an old married lady—and bring gifts for my children."

Why was she tormenting him this way? Was this the way to send him off to battle? He let go of her hand. "I'd better get my things. So long, Rae. Wish me luck." She murmured something in Arabic, but he couldn't quite catch it. He strode off without looking back. Her words had stung. It was hardly the farewell he had imagined.

When he emerged from the cabin with his pack, the captain called from the wharf that it was time to leave. Moises and the others called out their farewells and good wishes. Saul was already seated on the cart with the horse's reins in his hand. Alan glanced expectantly toward the bow, but Rae had gone. *An old married lady.* Had she intended all along to please her father and marry Jason? As he walked down the gangplank toward the cart, he wondered if he would ever see her again.

It was the worst possible moment for everything to end.

So much was at stake, with Hugo entrenched in the castle.

One fastening toward the rear of the cart was undone. Flipping up the tarpaulin, he saw that there was a fairly large space between the bolts of silk. He flung his pack into the cart, hoisted himself over the edge, and slid into the space. Once in, he flapped the tarpaulin closed and settled into the darkness.

"All set, Alan? Comfortable?"

"Fine." He heard the crack of a whip and the squeak of the wheels starting to turn. A moment later, as the cart jolted slowly over the cobblestones, the tarpaulin was flipped up again. A body fell over the cart's edge and rolled up against him.

Alan was startled. "What—?"

A finger was placed against his lips. "Shhh!"

"Rae! What're you doing here?"

"I couldn't let you go alone." Her lips were close to his ear. "I'm going to help you fight Hugo!"

Happiness rolled over him like a wave over the bow of the ship. "But the way you talked—when you said good-bye—I thought—"

She giggled. "You're supposed to be my bright pupil. You should've understood."

"But what'll your father say? And Charlemagne?"

She poked him in the ribs. "Nobody forbade me to go, did they? Besides, it'll be too late then!"

He laughed to himself at the image of Rae brandishing her scimitar. A sight even the Holy Roman Emperor

himself had never laid eyes on! Still, having her there would add to his worries. And he had plenty to worry about already. For one thing, he was in the dark about Charlemagne's plan. And what about his mother? He had no way of getting word to her that the action against Hugo and his henchmen was coming.

A deep sigh came from him. Rae rubbed her cheek against his, and he put his arm around her. They had never been this close before. It would take a couple of hours to get to Toulon. Having her so near him was incredible. He could hardly believe it.

Rae yawned. "Alan, I'm so sleepy. I hardly slept last night." Her lips grazed his and she yawned again.

He closed his eyes. "Me, neither." Entwined together, lulled by the creaking of the cart, they slept.

A jolt of the cart brought Alan awake. Rae was curled against him, fast asleep. His arm about her had grown numb. He slid it away slowly, so as not to disturb her. He clenched and unclenched his fist to get rid of the pins-and-needles sensation. He was on his way to confront his cousin at last. How would this day end? No matter. It was well worth trying, even if he died in the attempt. And if I do, he vowed to himself, I'll take Hugo with me.

Anyway, right now he was alive, and Rae was next to him. He smiled, nestled close to the comforting warmth of her body, and was instantly asleep again. The cart's rumbling to a stop woke him. Someone was speaking. "They're waiting for you inside, Captain." It was Jason.

"You there, old man, you can open the gates now."

"Yes, sir." Alan recognized Lothair's voice. It sent a pang through him. *Old Lothair, still there, thank God. Won't he be surprised when he sees me!*

Footsteps. Then Captain Isaac's voice next to the tarpaulin. "Alan? Don't come out till I call you. Understand?"

"Yes, Captain." Alan felt Rae stir and awaken. He put his finger against her lips to warn her. The cart rolled on for a minute more, then stopped. Alan waited until all the footsteps died away, then he nudged Rae. "Let's go." He lifted the tarpaulin and blinked at the daylight. Rae sat up, yawned, and stretched.

"Wait a minute." Alan looked about the courtyard. Empty. He nodded to Rae and sprang over the side, holding out his arms for her. She let him lower her to the ground. *Six months ago,* he thought, *she would've spurned my help.* The change from the air under the tarpaulin, warmed by their breath, to the wintry chill of the outside world made them pull their cloaks closer. A light mist was dampening their faces. Alan pointed toward the castle. "This way—side door."

There was no one guarding the door. It opened into a long corridor lit by wall sconces. The end of the corridor seemed brightly lit. Rae pointed. "What's down there?"

"It's the great hall. Follow me." He led the way, pausing before one of the side corridors to make sure it was

empty. When they got to the entrance of the great hall, Alan stationed himself at one side and motioned for Rae to stay hidden across the way.

What Alan saw when he peered around the edge of the entrance infuriated him. In the knight's chair, the chair where Gerard of Toulon had always sat, sprawled Hugo, flushed and self-important. Next to him sat Alan's mother. His first impulse was to leap out and embrace her. But that would wreck whatever plan the emperor had hatched. Then he noticed that Hugo had a silver cup in his hand. Alan's father's cup! Again, he had to squelch the urge to rush forward and bury his scimitar in that traitor's throat.

Instead, he concentrated on his mother. The countess seemed to be in good health, but her face had an air of sadness. Her fair hair was in disarray, and there were dark circles under her eyes. It was not hard to imagine what life had been like with Hugo in charge.

"Psst! Alan!" Rae's whisper came from across the way. "Look at the soldiers!"

How could he have not noticed? A circle of armed soldiers ringed the walls of the great hall. Obviously, Hugo had been raising an army. Alan looked about the hall again, trying to see if anything had been changed. A great fire roared in the massive fireplace. Torches and candles everywhere made the room bright. On Hugo's other side sat the stout bishop of Toulon, winecup in hand.

Wait, something was different. Why was the doorway

leading to the rear of the castle covered by a tapestry? He didn't remember that being there before. Alan suddenly realized that the captain was speaking. He was standing in the center of the room, flanked by Jason and Saul.

"Master Hugo, you'll be pleased to know that we've carried out your mission successfully. The cargo of silks and spices is outside."

Hugo took a gulp from the silver cup and wiped his lips on his sleeve. "You bring good news, Captain. But I'd like to see a sample, if you don't mind."

Captain Isaac turned to Jason and motioned toward the door. Jason left. That's torn it, thought Alan, he'll find I'm not in the cart. Jason returned, carrying a bolt of silk and two boxes, and whispered in the captain's ear.

Captain Isaac barely nodded. Taking the bolt from Jason, he spread the silk out on the table before Hugo. "The finest silk to be found in all of Persia." He opened one of the boxes and carried it to where Hugo sat. "Cinnamon, Master Hugo. The purest from the Far East. Here, smell."

Hugo bent forward and sniffed. "Hmmm. Is it as valuable as pepper?"

"Even rarer, Master Hugo, and worth much more."

Hugo took another sip from the cup and waved his hand. "Very well, I'll take the lot, Isaac."

Watching, Alan thought, Hugo's put on weight. His cheeks are bulging and so is his waistline. And his face is flushed. He always liked his drink a little too well.

The captain was speaking. "There's the matter of price, Master Hugo. The cost of the entire mission comes to two thousand gold livres."

Hugo frowned. "That's more than I expected to pay."

Captain Isaac shrugged and drew a piece of parchment from his tunic. "It's all written here. Besides the cost of the cargo, there's supplies for the voyage, pay for the crew, damages incurred during a storm, a camel caravan, and guides."

"Enough!" Hugo slammed the silver cup down on the table so hard that wine slopped over. "I don't think you got my meaning, Jew."

Alan's mother rose. "Hugo, please don't do this."

Hugo turned. "Keep out of this, woman! Let me remind you that you're only here by my charity! I'm in charge now! I make the decisions!" She gasped and sank back in her chair.

It was more than Alan could bear. Crying "You cowardly traitor!" he sprang into the center of the room and confronted Hugo. "She took you in and cared for you all those years!"

Behind him came Rae, scimitar in hand.

There were simultaneous outcries of their names from Alan's mother and Rae's father. Hugo jumped to his feet, shouting, "Seize them!" Before Alan and Rae could defend themselves, they were grabbed by half a dozen soldiers and disarmed. "Take the other three, also!" A few seconds later, Isaac, Saul, and Jason were also

prisoners.

The countess's eyes were wide. "Alan, is it really you? Hugo told me you were never coming back."

Hugo snorted. "So the Jew lied to me! You were hiding on his boat, weren't you, weakling?" He looked Alan up and down. "Well, you're taller, and you've got a man's beard. But that doesn't make you a man."

"Just give me the chance to prove it!"

"Maybe later, if I need a bit of sport. But I've got more important business at hand." He turned to Captain Isaac. "You see, Jew, what I intend to pay is nothing!"

The captain's eyebrows rose in mock astonishment. "Nothing? But it was a gentleman's agreement."

Hugo guffawed. "Our good bishop has something to tell you." He nodded toward the cleric.

The bishop of Toulon put down his cup and cleared his throat. "It seems, my dear captain, that you have been keeping something from us. Something that grieves us sorely." He narrowed his eyes. "Jew, you have broken one of the laws of the Church—that no Christian child shall be sold into slavery by any citizen of the Frankish Empire!"

"Christian children? Sold as slaves? That's nonsense!"

"Ah, not nonsense. Truth! And for this crime you shall pay the penalty. All your worldly possessions shall be forfeit!"

"Wait a minute!" cried the captain. "Where's the evidence?"

The bishop turned to Hugo with a smile. "The Jew wants evidence, Hugo. Shall we give it to him?"

Alan had expected the bishop's lies. But he had not expected that the Radanites would all be disarmed so quickly. How would they get out of this trap? Hadn't they realized how many soldiers would be guarding Hugo?

"Here is our evidence, Jew!" The bishop rose and marched over to the tapestry that closed off the back hallway. He waved his arm. "Behind this tapestry are the children. We managed to rescue them from your clutches. These innocents will tell of your wickedness!"

He reached over and yanked the tapestry aside.

✧ CHAPTER TWENTY ✧

ith a gasp, the bishop of Toulon fell back. His face, flushed from too many cups of wine, now paled. In the opening stood a tall, broad figure, magnificent in full battle dress. Watching, Alan caught his breath.

It was the emperor.

Charlemagne loomed over the stricken bishop, poking his long sword into the cleric's stomach. "Sorry to disappoint you. But the children you paid to stand here are all back safe in their homes."

"But—but—how—" The bishop's pouchy face sagged, his body drooped. He fell to his knees. "Mercy, Your Majesty, mercy!"

The astonished Hugo recovered quickly. He seized the long sword of the soldier next to him and brandished it. "Men," he shouted to his soldiers, "he's only one man alone! Take him!"

But the soldiers seemed hypnotized by the appearance of Charlemagne. They stood there, gawking.

Alan's voice broke the silence. He tore his arm away from his captor and pointed to Charlemagne. "That's your new emperor, men! We just sailed in from Rome—we saw the pope crown him Holy Roman Emperor!"

The soldiers looked at each other. Suddenly, one of them went down on one knee and bent his head. Another followed. Soon all of Hugo's men were kneeling on the floor in homage.

"You may rise." Charlemagne spoke in that booming voice that men knew and feared all over Europe. He eyed Hugo. "Nor am I here alone. This castle is now surrounded by my troops." He directed his attention to the soldiers. "Are you men willing to give up your allegiance to Hugo of Toulon? And join my army?"

A sergeant sprang up and saluted. "You can count us in, Your Majesty!"

"Good! Then I order you to take hold of this poor excuse for a bishop and Hugo there. At once! And give these people back their weapons!"

Alan sprang to his mother's side and embraced her. Tears wet their faces, as they clung together. She kissed him. "I thought you were dead, Alan! I wept for you

every night." She drew back and touched his cheek. "Look at you, a beard—a grown man."

At the same time, Saul was hugging Rae. A second later, he was scolding her. "You little idiot! Why did you come? You might've been killed!"

She brushed her hair from her forehead. "I couldn't let Alan face danger alone! I care about him! And you once told me that loyalty is more precious than jewels!"

Charlemagne's voice rang out again. "Bring Hugo before me!" The soldiers dragged Hugo over and thrust him to the floor before the emperor. "I find it hard to believe that the son of a noble family would engage in such a vicious plot!" Hugo's eyes widened. "Oh, yes, I know all about your dealings with Simon of Brittany. Part of my army is on its way right now to deal with him!"

Hugo opened his mouth, but closed it as Charlemagne pointed his sword at him. "Do not speak! Thanks to young Alan and Isaac the Radanite, I learned everything. We found the woodcutters you bribed to have their children chained as mock slaves."

He turned his attention to the bishop of Toulon. "And you, Bishop, a man of the cloth. What possessed you to join this man in such an odious scheme? You planned to incriminate my old friend, Captain Isaac! Why? Because he's a Jew? You, of all people, should know my law. On Frankish soil every citizen is treated alike!"

Hugo and the bishop stayed on their knees, heads bent, silent.

Charlemagne clapped his hands. "Take these two out-side and wait for me!"

"One moment, Your Majesty!" The captain spoke quietly. "There is still a score to be settled here."

Charlemagne motioned for the soldiers to wait. "What do you mean, Captain Isaac?"

"Alan of Toulon has more than one grievance against his cousin Hugo. First, Hugo's plan was to murder Alan and take over the castle. That was almost a year ago, when Alan was certainly not strong enough to defend himself. Second, before you came in, Hugo taunted the countess, Alan's mother, in her son's presence. Surely, Alan has the right to seek redress for all that has happened."

"There's more, Your Majesty!" The countess rose and pointed at Hugo. "My husband, Gerard of Toulon, died in a hunting accident, we thought. But that man actually boasted in a drunken fit that he had arranged the accident—"

She stopped as she saw the horrified look on Alan's face. "Oh, son, I hoped you'd never find out—"

"Never mind, Mother! I'm not the boy who ran off with the Radanites." He turned to Charlemagne. "Sir, I beg leave to challenge Hugo to a duel—here and now in your presence."

"A duel? Are you sure?" Alan saw Charlemagne look at the captain. Was that a wink that fluttered over Isaac's eye? "Very well. Perhaps justice will be better served.

You have my permission. Release the prisoner and give him back his sword."

"Wait!" The countess clutched Alan's arm. "Their weapons are not equal!"

"Don't worry, Mother." Alan leaned down and whispered, "I can take care of myself."

Charlemagne ordered the center of the room to be cleared. A circle formed about the two combatants, who stood apart from the center. Jason ran over to Alan and said something in a low voice. Alan nodded, and Jason slipped back to his place.

Alan tossed his cloak aside and looked over at Rae. She was mouthing words at him, but he couldn't make them out. He thrust the medallion that swung at his breast under his tunic. Perhaps it would be the talisman that would guide his arm.

Hugo seemed to have regained his bluster. He flourished his long sword. "Are you just going to use that toothpick, weakling?"

Alan raised his scimitar. "On your guard, Hugo."

The great hall was silent, waiting. It had all come full circle for Alan. The castle, Hugo and the bishop, his mother, his father's silver cup. Was this the moment he had been waiting for his entire life? He remembered Scheherazade's words and breathed deeply.

They circled each other warily, panthers stalking a kill. Hugo made the first move. He leaped toward Alan, swinging his long sword with the same mighty slashes that in

the past always drove Alan back against the wall.

The countess leaned forward, gripping the arms of her chair. Her mouth opened, as she saw Alan managing to dodge the first swipes of the sword. Alan tried to engage the long sword with his blade. A mistake. The point of Hugo's sword caught the scimitar near the hilt and ripped it out of Alan's hand. Hugo's eyes lit up with the gleam of victory.

"Alan, catch!" The cry from Rae's throat alerted Alan. The hilt of her scimitar sailed through space toward him. He grabbed it and managed to parry the swipe of the long sword aimed at his neck.

Now Hugo changed his tactics and lunged, aiming for Alan's heart. The point of his sword struck Alan's chest and made him lose his balance. He crashed to the floor. Hugo lifted his arm for the finishing blow.

The countess screamed and started out of her chair. She sank back as Alan, dazed to find himself still alive, rolled away. Hugo's blade crunched a sliver out of the wooden floor. Rae cried out, ready to come to Alan's rescue. Saul restrained her.

Alan scrambled to his feet. He expected to be pierced by Hugo's lunge. But a quick glance showed him that there was no blood on his tunic. And he felt no pain. What kept Hugo's sword from piercing his chest? The caliph's medallion under his tunic? As he and Hugo circled each other, Alan touched the talisman once more.

Hugo attacked again. This time his slashes came down

at an angle, carving out figure eights. With agile leaps to one side, Alan used his scimitar to make Hugo's weapon slide by harmlessly.

Out of breath from his exertions with the heavy weapon, Hugo stopped slashing and staggered back. He seemed dazed by his inability to cut Alan in two. Alan seized this moment to make his move. His scimitar came down from on high toward Hugo's head. Hugo raised his sword to parry the blow. Just before the scimitar struck steel, Alan reversed the motion of his swing. His scimitar swooped up under the sword and slashed through cloth to pierce the forearm of the hand holding the long sword.

Blood gushed out to stain the sleeve of Hugo's tunic. He uttered a cry of pain. The long sword dropped from his fingers. In a flash, the point of Alan's scimitar was at Hugo's throat.

"Kneel, you snake!" Hugo slid to his knees, clutching the sleeve of his wounded arm. "Any reason you shouldn't die?"

"I'm hurt, Alan!" In his upturned face, tears came to Hugo's eyes. "Remember, I'm your cousin. We're family. You can't kill me!"

Alan pushed the scimitar point a little deeper into Hugo's neck. "I didn't hear much about family that night up on the battlements—when you and the bishop were busy plotting to do away with me!"

"A mistake!" Hugo pointed to the bishop. "It was his crazy idea. He's a madman! He talked me into it!"

"And did he talk you into killing my father? What did you do, put a burr under his saddle to make his horse throw him? Just what a coward would do!" The point went a little deeper. A spot of blood appeared on Hugo's neck. "The truth, Hugo, the truth!"

"So what if I did? Yes, I did fix the saddle! It was the bishop's idea. What are you going to do about it? Kill me?" A vein throbbed in Hugo's neck. "Go ahead, if you can!"

"You murderer!" Alan drew his scimitar back for the death blow. He'd dreamed so long about this moment.

"Alan, stop!" The countess rushed over and grasped his upraised arm. "There's been enough death in this castle. Don't kill him! Leave him to His Majesty's justice!"

Alan looked into his mother's eyes. How could he do anything that would add to the despair she had suffered? He lowered his scimitar and turned to Charlemagne. "He's yours, Your Majesty."

Tears flowing down her cheeks, the countess embraced her son. "If only your father could've been here today to see you!"

"So as well as treason, there'll be a charge of murder." Charlemagne motioned to the soldiers. Hugo and the bishop were dragged out. The emperor beckoned Alan to come before him. "By God, that was well fought, young Alan!"

Alan turned toward Jason. "I owe that skill to my teacher."

Charlemagne nodded. "Ah, those Radanites! Very wise of you, too, to heed your mother's words. It takes a true man to curb the desire for revenge. And with those charges against him, I doubt you need worry about Hugo anymore." He put his hand on Alan's shoulder. "Kneel before me, Alan of Toulon."

Alan bent his knee and bowed. The emperor cleared his throat. "Alan, count of Toulon, I am indebted to you for revealing this traitor's plot." He drew his sword and tapped Alan on each shoulder. "I dub thee, Alan, baron of Toulon. For your service, more lands will be added to those already in your family's name. You may rise."

"Your Majesty, I will serve you faithfully all the years of my life, just as my father, Gerard, did."

"Thank you." Charlemagne bowed to the countess. "Farewell, Madame. We have started the new year well, thanks to your son." To the captain, he said, "Shall I expect you in Marseilles?"

"Harun-al-Rashid's gifts will be delivered to your quarters, Your Majesty."

Charlemagne waved gracefully to the group and did an about-face. He marched out, followed by the soldiers who had once been loyal to Hugo.

"Well, *Baron* Alan of Toulon," said Captain Isaac with a smile. "Now that you're such an elevated nobleman, I hope you'll condescend to do business with an old friend once in a while?"

Alan grasped his hand. "How can I ever thank you?"

Rae ran over, disregarding Saul's frown, to throw her arms around Alan and kiss him. "You were wonderful!" She laughed. "But you've got to get a better grip on that scimitar!"

He hugged her close. Finally he drew back to hand her her scimitar. "I owe you my life."

She flourished her scimitar in the air. "If that rat had hurt you, I would've run him through like this!"

Alan laughed. "I could feel you cheering me on all the while."

"Nothing could've stopped me from coming with you! But I still have to make my peace with my father." She sighed and walked back to Saul.

In a serious voice, Alan spoke to Isaac. "Captain, I've thought a lot lately about my future. I wanted to give up being a Christian knight and become a Radanite. But now, back home, I'm not sure."

The captain shook his head. "Alan, that's a great compliment. But it's not easy to turn from the faith of your father. You have to think of your mother, too. So for now, keep your own religion." He cut his speech short. "Oh, about the goods in the cart—"

"Hugo's mission? What about it?"

"Well, I really didn't pay you a full share for your service aboard the *Devora*. So why don't you keep a part of the cargo instead?"

"But, Captain," Alan protested. "It's too valuable."

"No, no, take it. We Radanites share and share alike."

"But you really saved me."

"Alan," said his mother, "don't argue with the captain! It's very kind of him. Besides, we'll need money to rebuild. Hugo let things go terribly while you were away."

Alan shrugged. "Looks like I'm outvoted. Thank you, Captain Isaac."

"My pleasure. Well, come on, Saul, Jason, Rae. Let's get Alan's share out of the wagon. We've got to get started."

Jason came forward and pressed Alan's hand. "Nice going, pupil! You made all the right moves." Saul, too, shook his hand and said, "Well done!"

Before Rae's father could turn away, Alan said, "Sir, I'd like to ask a favor. My mother's been under the thumb of that villain for such a long time. A little company would be good medicine for her. Can Rae stay here in the castle as our guest for a while?"

Saul frowned and stood pursing his lips, but Rae's face glowed. She put her hand on his. "Oh, Father, can I? I've never lived in a castle before! And I'll behave like a lady, I promise! Please, Father, please say yes!"

Alan's mother came up to Saul. "Sir, we haven't been introduced."

"Mother, this is Saul, the bos'n of Captain Isaac's ship. And this is Rachel, my shipmate. She's his daughter."

"Your daughter is welcome to be our guest for as long as she likes. And I will see to it that she lacks nothing."

Saul shifted from one foot to another. "You don't

understand, Countess. Our Radanite ways are different."

"If you mean that you are Jews, then have no fears, sir. When my husband was alive, we often had Jewish guests. I know well the forbidden foods, which were never served to them here. Let me add my invitation to that of my son." To Rae she said, "My dear, do you know how to embroider?"

Rae looked bewildered.

"I'll teach you everything." The countess was bright with anticipation.

Rae rolled her eyes at Alan. He winked back.

Captain Isaac put his hand on Saul's shoulder. "Forgive me for meddling, Saul. But can your daughter spend her whole life aboard ship? She's not a child anymore. Once I thought I knew what was best for my son, Reuben. And I lost him."

Saul looked at him, then at the countess, then at Rachel's pleading face. He stood a minute, rubbing his chin with his knuckles. "Well, Captain, perhaps you're right." He eyed Jason. "How about you, Jason, is it all right with you?"

"All right with me?" Jason slammed a fist into his other hand. "Saul, a promise is a promise! Rae and I have been pledged to marry since we were children. Don't ask me for my blessing!"

Rae confronted him. "Jason, listen to me. All of that is ancient history. This is a new country, things are different now! Women have minds of their own. You know

that I'll always care for you. You're my brother." She gave him a warm hug.

Jason released her with a sigh. "I suppose I'll have to be satisfied with that. No man wants an unwilling bride."

Saul scratched his beard. "What can I do, Rachel, lock you up and throw away the key? Very well, you may stay. For the time being, at least. Then we'll see. But if I hear any rumors...."

Rachel gave Saul a demure look. "Why, Father, you know that I always behave myself!" She reached up and kissed Saul's cheek. "Thank you."

After the good-byes, Alan called out, "Captain Isaac, when will we meet again?"

The captain turned. His face broke into a grin. "Alan, when the caliph gave you that medallion, you became an honorary Radanite. You're welcome to voyage with us at any time."

"Even to Cathay?"

"Even to the ends of the earth!"

As the Radanites left, the countess asked, "Medallion? What medallion was he talking about?"

"Wait'll you hear, Countess." Rae locked arms with the countess. "It happened in Baghdad."

Watching his mother and Rae, Alan thought, everything's perfect. Well, not altogether. Later I'll visit my father's grave on the hill. And ask his forgiveness for not having gone hunting with him that terrible day. But at least I can tell him that at last I've beaten Hugo. With

a Moorish scimitar.

There was a sudden commotion at the side door. Alan heard a kind of mixed whine and bark. Lothair appeared, grinning broadly and holding a chain, which he then let go.

At once Alan was bowled over by a big brown dog, who alternated between tongue-washing his face and yelping shrill barks of joy.

"Brunhilde! You remember me!"

Wrapping his arms around the dog, Alan wrestled on the floor with her. Then he sat up and motioned to Rae. "Come meet Brunhilde." He nuzzled the dog. "This is a special guest, Brunhilde, treat her well." Brunhilde sniffed at Rae's proffered hand and obediently gave it the lick of friendship.

"She likes you!" The countess smiled. "Such a clever dog! Oh, it's wonderful to have life in the castle again! Rachel, why don't I show you to your room?"

Rae put her hand to her mouth. "Oh, I forgot. All my clothes and things are back on the *Devora*."

Alan jumped up. "They're probably still out there unloading. Don't worry, I'll get them to send your things." He started out of the room, Brunhilde frisking at his heels. Then he stopped and eyed Rae. In a teacher's solemn voice, he said, "I have an announcement!

"It's too cold for swimming right now. But astronomy lessons begin tonight—up on the battlements!"

AFTERWORD

This is a work of fiction. Many of the characters in it, as well as the happenings, are inventions of the storytellers' minds. But this story was created around the few facts we know about the time during which our tale takes place.

We know that the Radanites existed. It is thought that their name came from the Hebrew term *rah dan,* meaning "trade routes." When this group of merchant Jews became sailors and how long they worked at this profession are unknown. They are mentioned only briefly in the writings of some travelers of the ninth century.

We know that King Charlemagne did send a Radanite, "Isaac the Jew," to Baghdad as an envoy of peace, bearing gifts. He did bring back a white baby elephant to Charlemagne's palace at Aachen. There is historical evidence that Isaac performed this errand around the year A.D. 800, and that it took him about four years to make the round trip. But we have shortened the time sequence for Captain Isaac in this story. After all, the great Greek historian Xenophon records that Cyrus the Great was able to march his army 270 miles along the Euphrates River in the Arabian Desert in 13 days!

Harun-al-Rashid was the caliph at Baghdad at that time. He, too, wished to be at peace with the Christian world. In addition to the elephant, he gave Charlemagne the city of Jerusalem, so that Christian pilgrims could travel there without fear of being killed. The Mediterranean Sea

was not really open to Christian shipping. Arab pirates abounded, ready to seize cargoes and take seamen as slaves. It was a time when slavery was an accepted social condition in all civilized countries. The Radanites, apparently, were one group that may have had the freedom to sail the Mediterranean without fear of being attacked. No one knows why. They followed the trade routes not only to Baghdad, but to India and even as far as China.

Harun is also said to be the caliph of the time of the famous collection of Arab folktales, *The Arabian Nights,* in which the slave girl, Scheherazade, manages to stay alive by telling her ruler one story each night for one thousand and one nights. As a reward, he makes her a princess. We are all familiar with some of the stories, like "Aladdin and the Magic Lamp." Still, we don't know if there really was a Scheherazade, or if she is only a figment of the imagination of a storyteller.

We trust the reader will not fret over the liberties we have taken with the facts of history. For example, we don't really know how Charlemagne spent the week after his coronation. But we do know that he did often join forces with his noblemen in order to retain his power. So while this story is fictional, it is within the realm of possibility and works within the known facts to a certain extent. More important, we hope that the adventures of Alan of Toulon give the reader a picture of life in those times.